PENGUIN

R.U.R. (ROSSUM'S UNIVERSAL ROBOTS)

KAREL ČAPEK (1890–1938) was born in Bohemia, part of Austria at the time, and majored in biology at the Caroline University in Prague. He was the stage manager of the theater in Vinohrady and married to a prominent actress. Although a prominent journalist and advocate of democracy, he is best known for *R.U.R.* and his novel, *War With the Newts.* His later works deal with the rise of dictatorship and the consequences of war, and he died on Christmas Day, shortly before the Nazi invasion of Czechoslovakia.

CLAUDIA NOVACK has a Ph.D. in Slavic Linguistics from Brown University, where she received the Presidential Award for Excellence in Teaching. She currently teaches in the Department of Chemistry at Brandeis University.

IVAN KLÍMA was born in 1931 and survived the Terezin concentration camp. His work was long suppressed under Communism, and most was first published outside his home country. He is a renowned award-winning novelist, playwright, and essayist, and lives in Prague.

KAREL ČAPEK

R.U.R.

(ROSSUM'S UNIVERSAL ROBOTS)

Translated by CLAUDIA NOVACK
Introduction by IVAN KLÍMA

PENGUIN BOOKS

PENGUIN BOOKS
Published by the Penguin Group
Penguin Group (USA) Inc., 375 Hudson Street, New York, New York 10014, U.S.A.
Penguin Group (Canada), 90 Eglinton Avenue East, Suite 700, Toronto, Ontario,
Canada M4P 2Y3 (a division of Pearson Penguin Canada Inc.)
Penguin Books Ltd, 80 Strand, London WC2R 0RL, England
Penguin Ireland, 25 St Stephen's Green, Dublin 2, Ireland (a division of Penguin Books Ltd)
Penguin Group (Australia), 250 Camberwell Road, Camberwell, Victoria 3124, Australia
(a division of Pearson Australia Group Pty Ltd)
Penguin Books India Pvt Ltd, 11 Community Centre, Panchsheel Park,
New Delhi – 110 017, India
Penguin Group (NZ), 67 Apollo Drive, Rosedale, North Shore 0632,
New Zealand (a division of Pearson New Zealand Ltd)
Penguin Books (South Africa) (Pty) Ltd, 24 Sturdee Avenue, Rosebank,
Johannesburg 2196, South Africa

Penguin Books Ltd, Registered Offices: 80 Strand, London WC2R 0RL, England

First published in Penguin Books 2004

23 25 27 29 30 28 26 24

Translation copyright © Claudia Novack, 2004
Introduction copyright © Ivan Klíma, 2004
All rights reserved

Originally published in Prague by Aventinum, 1921.

Ms. Novack's translation appeared in somewhat different form in *Toward the Radical Center:
A Karel Čapek Reader*, edited by Peter Kussi, Catbird Press, 1990.

CAUTION: In this present form, this play is dedicated to the reading public only. Professional and amateur
performance, motion picture, and radio and television broadcasting rights, as well as the right to translate
into foreign languages are strictly reserved to the translator, Claudia Novack. Address all inquiries
concerning performance and production rights of any kind to Claudia Novack, c/o Catbird Press,
16 Windsor Road, North Haven, CT 06473.

LIBRARY OF CONGRESS CATALOGING IN PUBLICATION DATA
Čapek, Karel, 1890-1938.
[R.U.R. English]
R.U.R. (Rossum's Universal Robots)/ Karel Capek ; translated by Claudia Novack ;
introduction by Ivan Klíma.
p.   cm.—(Penguin classics)
ISBN 978-0-14-118208-7
I. Novack, Claudia.   II. Title.   III. Series.
PG5038.C3R213 2004
891.8'6252—dc22   2003061698

Printed in the United States of America
Set in Sabon

Contents

Introduction

Few members of the younger Czech generation realize that some two hundred years ago only a minority of their ancestors spoke Czech. Within the lands of the Bohemian crown, the aristocracy spoke Italian, French, and German, and the townspeople exclusively spoke German, while the clergy spoke German and, of course, Latin. Czech was spoken only in the villages. Czech literature, insofar as contemporary writing deserved that term, had only local significance. The land could not boast of a single author, whether writing in Czech or German, whose work penetrated beyond its frontiers. It was only in the nineteenth century, with the rapid development of industry and the end of serfdom and bondage, that the rural population began to settle in towns, often bringing with them their sole property: the Czech language. In the course of several decades, aided by the fervor of the so-called "national awakeners," Czech made increasing inroads into Prague and other German-speaking towns.

It was only then that Czech literature was born. However, its creators quite logically considered it their first task to develop and perfect the language and make it capable of expressing even complicated ideas. They invented a whole array of new terms, and became enthusiastic propagators of folk literature as a source of national pride and muse. Since most early Czech authors came from rural regions, another major source of inspiration was the life of country people, their wisdom and philosophic outlook, understandably of a basically conservative cast.

Urban experience did not play a major part in Czech literature until the second half of the nineteenth century, notably with the work of Jan Neruda, who expressed new kinds of experience, new human relationships, and a different way of regarding life. His generation was obsessed with the goal of producing literature comparable to that of their colleagues in highly cultured countries. Many Czech writers were also outstanding translators, enabling Czech readers to become familiar with the great works of world literature.

During the nineteenth century, Czech literature thus passed through a course of development that had taken hundreds of years in other countries. Members of the last generation born in the nineteenth century such as Jaroslav Hašek, author of *The Good Soldier Švejk* and born in 1883, reached their artistic maturity in the twentieth. Another member of this generation was Karel Čapek.

Karel Čapek was born in January of 1890 in a small town in Northern Bohemia, where his father was the local doctor. He was the youngest of three siblings, all of whom proved to be artistically gifted. The oldest, Helena, became a writer and Josef became especially prominent as one of the most remarkable modern Czech painters. Karel, too, had some graphic talents and illustrated many of his own books—especially his travel books—with original, witty drawings.

All three Čapeks left their home quite early. Karel and Josef went to Prague, which at that time was already an important cultural and educational center with a number of prominent scholars (for instance, Albert Einstein taught at the German branch of the University). Above all, the young Čapeks were drawn to the modern architects and artists who began to flourish in Prague. Karel began to study philosophy and aesthetics, while collaborating with his brother on witty, ironic, and instructive prose pieces published under the name "The Čapek Brothers." Karel also began to contribute critical articles on art and literature to newspapers, marking the start of his lifelong involvement with journalism. As was customary in those days, he embarked on a study tour abroad and spent some time at the Sorbonne, where he devoted himself to the study of

Germanic culture. But above all, he chose "this holy Grail of artists"—as he referred to Paris—in order to spend time in galleries, cafes, and book shops and to savor Parisian life in the company of other artists and bohemians.

Nothing phenomenal had happened in his young life, not even a love affair. He could have expected a successful career as a writer or philosopher, but it is hard to judge what his future might have been if the catastrophic event that deeply marked his generation had not taken place. World War I, totally unexpected by most, was the greatest and bloodiest war the world had ever seen, a war featuring all the inventions of modern science and technology: bombs, poison gas, machine guns, airplanes, tanks.

Čapek suffered from an ailment of the spinal vertebrae, later diagnosed as Bechterew's disease, and was declared unfit for military service. Though he did not suffer from the food shortages rampant in Prague, thanks to help from his parents, as with most members of his generation, the cruel, senseless carnage of war shattered the world of certainties: the commonly shared illusion that by means of unprecedented technical progress, civilization was moving toward a better, easier life.

Many writers and other intellectuals returned from the war with a sharp awareness of their responsibility for charting a new course for humanity, ensuring that the horrors of wartime would never again be repeated. Of course, conclusions drawn by artists from their wartime experiences were often contradictory. A sizeable part of the European intelligentsia, influenced by Marxist thought as well as revolutionary events in Russia, came to believe that the war was caused by the greed and arrogance of international capital. They therefore thought it necessary to put a violent end to the capitalist system and to start building a more humane society based on socialist or even communist ideals.

Čapek's conclusions from his wartime experience were ambivalent.

Aside from horrors, the World War gave the Czechs an independent republic, larger even than the dimensions of the historic Czech lands. Čapek saw national independence within a

democratic framework as a basic precondition for the development of society, as an opportunity that history offered his
generation, and also as an obligation to use this opportunity
wisely for the benefit of upcoming generations. Through his
remarkable creative output, Čapek became the leading representative of democratic Czech culture. Through his literary
contributions, outstanding political commentaries, thousands
of newspaper articles, and excellent feuilletons and columns,
he expressed his views on the issues of contemporary civilization. By means of his political articles and essays, he conducted
polemics against the ideas of the two most dangerous ideolo-
gies of the twentieth century, ideas that endangered democracy
as well as the humanistic tradition of European culture: Soviet
Communism and German National Socialism.

Čapek was philosophically influenced by Pragmatism, which
enjoyed considerable attention at the time, especially in the
United States. Pragmatists such as William James and John
Dewey placed great emphasis upon the relativity of human
knowledge and attitudes, and therefore also upon the relativity
of the so-called great truths, religious and ideological. This basic supposition led them to resist all generations, all monumental visions to save the world. They maintained that what the
world needed was not great truths but tolerance—the idea that
someone who defends concepts and attitudes differing from
one's own may nevertheless be a good person who may have
discovered a useful truth.

Čapek had already been introduced to the ideas of Pragmatism during the war, through the lectures of Dr. Edvard Beneš
(who later became the second president of Czechoslovakia). As
a writer, Čapek found this philosophy congenial because it
explained various social conflicts primarily through human
psychology—people's intolerance and their attempts to simplify
generalizations. He therefore made a number of the Pragmatists' theses his own, and he believed that their general accep-
tance could dissolve the causes of social conflicts and prevent
violent attempts to solve these conflicts. He developed his ideas
in a number of essays, and some of his prose pieces and dramas
seem virtually like attempts to illustrate his Pragmatist thought.

For the youthful writer, the first four postwar years were a time of feverish activity. He worked as a journalist, first for the right-wing newspaper *Národní listy*, and then after 1921 for the liberal *Lidové noviny*, which, thanks to him, ultimately became the most serious of the Czech dailies. At the same time, he became the resident playwright of the prominent Czech theater in Vinohrady; and wrote the plays *The Robber, R.U.R., The Makropoulos Secret*, and the satiric comedy *From the Life of the Insects*, which he wrote with his brother. A collection of short stories, *Painful Tales*, was published, as was the utopian novel *The Absolute at Large*; and newspapers published his highly original "apocryphal tales."

However, it was a single play that gained world attention for Čapek almost overnight. *R.U.R.*, a collection drama featuring a "comic introductory section" and three acts, was finished in the spring of 1920 and given its premiere performance in Prague's National Theater in early 1921.

R.U.R. presented a theme extremely unusual for its time: an artificial human being, a brilliant worker, a Robot deprived of all "unnecessary" qualities: feelings, creativity, and the capacity for feeling pain. In *R.U.R.*, Robots gradually take over all the work and duties of people, even their military obligations. Čapek asked what such a revolutionary invention would do to humanity.

In the fall of 1908, the Čapek brothers jointly published a short story titled "The System," which had already introduced the basic idea of *R.U.R.*, even sketching out the essence of the play's plot. In this story, manufacturer John Andrew Ripraton explains his approach to solving the problems of labor and the organization of large-scale production:

> The world is nothing but raw material. The world is no more than unexploited matter. The sky and the earth, people, time and space and infinity, everything is just raw material. Gentlemen, the task of industry is to exploit the entire world . . . Everything must be speeded up. The labor question is holding us back . . . The worker must become a machine, so that he can simply rotate

like a wheel. Every thought is insubordination! Gentlemen! Tay-
lorism is systematically incorrect, because it disregards the question of a soul. A worker's soul is not a machine, therefore it must
be removed. This is my system . . . I have sterilized the worker,
purified him; I have destroyed in him all feelings of altruism and
camaraderie, all familial, poetic and *transcendental* feelings . . .

Just as in *R.U.R.*, the story extends *ad adsurdum* the ratio-
nalization of manufacture, turning man into a small part of a
complicated manufacturing mechanism and thereby reaching
maximum productivity. But dehumanization and rationaliza-
tion can be carried only so far. As soon as the workers grasp
their situation, they revolt and destroy the system. That's how
the 1908 short story ends.

The drama *R.U.R.* extends the problem much further, presenting onstage a truly perfect incarnation of a worker, stripped
of anything inessential to the manufacturing process. The artificial worker is more productive than the human, and is fully
capable of replacing his human counterpart, which deprives
human life of much of its meaning. This is manifested, among
other signs, by women's inability to bear children.

Čapek was evidently amused by developing his fantastic
theme, but above all, *R.U.R.* demonstrates the dangers of
grandiose visions that offer salvation, well-being, and good
fortune, that in reality yield only frustration and, finally, total
destruction. In the play, the chief proponent of this vision is the
director of the Robot factory, Domin. The human workers may
be out of work, "but within the next ten years Rossum's Universal Robots will produce so much wheat, so much cloth, so
much everything that things will no longer have any value.
Everyone will be able to take as much as he needs. There'll be
no more poverty. Yes, people will be out of work, but by then
there'll be no work left to be done. Everything will be done by
living machines. People will do only what they enjoy. They will
live only to perfect themselves."

To oppose the realization of this grandiose vision, Čapek
created a hero who defends traditional human values, the architect Alquist: "God, enlighten Domin and all those who err.

Destroy their work and help people to return to their former worries and labor. Protect the human race from destruction; do not permit harm to befall their bodies or souls. Rid us of the Robots . . ."

It was always important to Karel Čapek that his works, whether plays or prose fiction, give people some generally formulated message about the state of the world, civilization, society. There are few authors in world literature who accompany almost every one of their works with such commentaries. And no work of Čapek's contains more extensive explication than *R.U.R.*

It may seem like a paradox, but Čapek's interpretations cannot always be relied upon as fully trustworthy explanations. Čapek was drawn to fantastic themes, exotic environments, gripping plots—and critics generally considered these signs of second-rate creativity. Čapek therefore always emphasized the philosophic or noetic side of his work. In addition, in private life he was similar to Franz Kafka in that he was a shy person who shrank from presenting his personal problems before the public.

In this respect, it is interesting to note Čapek's remarks in *The Saturday Review* of July 23, 1923. It represents Čapek's reactions to the debate that took place in England following the premiere of *R.U.R.* Among the prominent figures participating in the debate were G. B. Shaw and G. K. Chesterton.

I wished to write a comedy, partly of science, partly of truth. The old inventor, Mr. Rossum, is no more or less than a typical representative of the scientific materialism of the last century. His desire to create an artificial man—in the chemical and biological, not the mechanical sense—is inspired by a foolish and obstinate wish to prove God unnecessary and meaningless. Young Rossum is the modern scientist, untroubled by metaphysical ideas; for him, scientific experiment is the road to industrial production; he is not concerned about proving, but rather manufacturing. To create a homunculus is a medieval idea; to bring it in line with the present century, this creation must be undertaken on the principle of mass production. We are in the grip of industrialism;

this terrible machinery must not stop, for if it does it would destroy the lives of thousands. It must, on the contrary, go on faster and faster, even though in the process it destroys thousands and thousands of lives . . . A product of the human brain has at last escaped from the control of human hands. This is the comedy of science.

These words precisely delineate the author's intention. In his work Čapek repeatedly returns to the theme of mass production, to the reality that man is coming to serve machines, rather than the opposite. When he visited the grandiose British Empire Exhibition in the summer of 1924, Čapek's comments were more than skeptical: "The only perfection of which modern civilization is capable is mechanical; machines are beautiful and perfect, but life which serves them or is served by them doesn't get any more beautiful or shiny or perfect or attractive . . ."

Of course, in *R.U.R.* Čapek didn't content himself merely with demonstrating that industrialism involved destructive tendencies. In the aforementioned commentary in *The Saturday Review,* he continued:

And now for my second idea, the comedy about truth. General director Domin tries to prove in the play that technical developments liberate man from heavy physical labor, and he is right. Alquist, the Tolstoyan architect, believes on the contrary that technical developments demoralize man, and I think that he is right, too. Busman thinks that only industrialism is capable of meeting modern needs; he is right. Helena instinctively fears all this human machinery, and she is quite right. And finally, the Robots themselves revolt against all these idealisms, and it seems that they are right as well.

We don't need to look for names for all these various antithetical idealisms. What I want to stress is that no matter whether these people are conservatives or socialists, yellow or red, all of them are right in a simple moral sense of the word. All of them have the most serious of motives, material and spiritual, for their beliefs, and according to their nature look for the greatest happiness for the greatest number of their fellows. I ask myself: isn't it possible to see in the contemporary social conflicts taking place in the world an analogous struggle between two, three or five equally serious and noble idealisms? I believe that it is possible. The most dramatic element in modern civilization is the fact that one human truth stands against a truth no less human, one ideal against another ideal, one positive value against a value no less positive, and that the conflict does not represent, as we are often told, a struggle between a noble truth and vile, selfish evil.

In this explanation of the play's second intention, it isn't difficult to detect the sound of relativistic philosophy. Everyone has his own truth. Even those whose actions seem to spring from quite opposite attitudes and interests may be acting out of totally idealistic motives. Čapek tried to explain the meaning of some of his other works along similar lines, including his comedy *The Robber,* and above all *The Absolute at Large,* written shortly after the production of *R.U.R.*

Yet insofar as Karel Čapek really had such creative intentions, who could have prevented their accomplishment? Most likely, only he himself. Shortly after the war Čapek prophetically sensed the deviousness of communist attitudes, and in spite of his relativistic convictions conducted passionate polemics against them, mainly because the communists claimed to have the sole valid truth about history and the solution of contemporary society's problems.

R.U.R. unmistakably sounds like a harsh condemnation of technocratic vision. Čapek did not place all the truths on the same level; he favored conservatism and Tolstoyan Alquist, as he himself dubbed him. And what could be a better demonstration of the falsity of Domin's grandiose vision than the fact that it led to the complete destruction of humanity? At the moment of humanity's total annihilation, it is irrelevant that all the play's figures had been motivated by sincere faith in their own truths. In the words of the popular proverb, the road to hell is paved with good intentions. Čapek's vision of total destruction overshadowed the thesis that everyone has his own noble truth.

What was it about this play by an author from a small country that aroused worldwide attention? Undoubtedly, what intrigued viewers the most was the play's utopian element. The word *Robot* (invented by Čapek's brother Josef) was adopted by many languages as an incarnation of the technical revolution. Artificial people without souls, without feelings—"machines" with human faces—had a very suggestive effect on stage. By creating his Robots, Čapek also showed great technical prescience. He endowed the Robots not only with physical capabilities but with a perfect memory. "If you were to read them a twenty-volume encyclopedia they could repeat the contents in order, but they never think up anything original." This characteristic certainly fits today's computers, an invention totally unexpected when *R.U.R.* was written.

Of course, in an era filled with social upheavals, revolution in Russia and revolutionary attempts in Hungary and Germany, the Robots also seemed to symbolize suppressed, revolting workers. And finally, there was the vision of a catastrophic war or uprising that annihilates mankind, a theme to which Čapek was to return in his novels *The Absolute at Large* and the outstanding novel *War with the Newts*. In the period following a terrible war, this vision of annihilation must have appeared to audiences all over the world as quite timely. Near the close of the second act of *R.U.R.*, a handful of basically defenseless people faces an overwhelming majority of armed Robots. Nowadays, this scene may seem somewhat over-dramatic, but to contemporary audiences it must have evoked scenes of trapped and defenseless people (including the Czar's family) who were mercilessly murdered in the Russian civil war.

From his childhood on, Čapek seemed to suffer from some kind of phobia related to encirclement, and scenes of siege are common in his work. This is especially striking in his drama *The Robber* and in his most lengthy novel, *Krakatit*. In his fiction, Čapek always stood on the side of the besieged, and he even sympathized with a murderer who is surrounded by an overwhelming force of policemen. One member of Čapek's generation, the translator Mathesius, left an interesting comment regarding Čapek's eccentric interest:

Čapek suddenly stopped, waved his cane and full of unusual excitement recounted an incident which at that time—April, 1912—gained the attention of the press throughout the world. The incident concerned the siege of a criminal hide-out by the police. If I can trust my notes from that period, two Paris gangsters were besieged in a garage of a French village, where they held out for an hour and a half against a superior police force. Čapek learned all the details from French newspapers and even drew for me a map of the garage and its surroundings in the sand.

According to Mathesius, Čapek was on the lookout for similar scenes and was delighted when he found a newspaper account of a murderer besieged in London's Whitechapel, who "held out all night against a thousand policemen and soldiers equipped with three cannons."

Čapek himself considered the scene dealing with a handful of bravely resisting people as crucial to his play. Several days after its premiere he wrote:

I admit . . . that I was seduced into writing the play by its plot, especially the two acts in which a handful of people, their heads held high, await their end; human heroism is among my beloved ideas and lured me to this material. And no matter what seems to flow from the finished work, I remained faithful to this idea . . . I wasn't concerned about Robots, but about people. If there was anything I thought exhaustively about in constructing the play, it was the fate of the six or seven people who were supposed to represent humanity. Yes, it was my passionate wish that at the moment of the robots' attack, the audience felt that something valuable and great was at stake, namely humanity, mankind, us. That "us" was all-important, that was the leading idea, that was the vision, the real program of the entire work . . . I wanted to show by means of a small group of people, within the brief space of two or three hours, what humanity was all about. It is hard for us to think of humanity as a dying or dead race. Yet imagine yourself standing at the grave of mankind; even the most extreme pessimist would surely realize the divine significance of this extinct species, and say: it was a great thing, to be human.

But no matter what his original intention in writing *R.U.R.* may have been, audiences and critics alike were fascinated by the idea of an artificial human, and by the consequences of this revolutionary—and still quite fantastic—invention. They considered the play utopian, or, as we would say today, "science fiction." The author encouraged this viewpoint by placing the action of the play around the year 2000 (this was stated in the Czech poster announcing the play's opening in January 1921) and by devoting so much attention to the technical explanation of his artificially created, mass-produced creatures.

On the other hand, perhaps audiences and critics were unduly influenced by the eerie appearance of the Robots. Was the play really a consistent utopia? After all, it is supposed to take place at a time when the Robot epoch has already reached its peak, and technical advances surely didn't come to a halt at the beginning of the twentieth century. The surrounded inhabitants of the island are totally dependent upon the arrival of the postal ship to communicate with the rest of the world. Čapek doesn't seem to take airplanes into account at all.

Although we find inconsistencies, it would be unfair to suspect an author as knowledgeable and logical as Čapek of being unaware of them. After all, in *The Absolute at Large,* he describes the use of energy derived from the splitting of the atom, and two years later he wrote an excellent fantasy novel, *Krakatit,* which deals with a destructive explosive again created through atomic fission and detonated by means of radio waves. Rather, he simply didn't find it important to think through the technical details of next century's life; in other words, to create science fiction.

But if we don't categorize the play as science fiction, how are we to understand it?

Čapek himself designated the play as a collective drama. At the time when *R.U.R.* was created, plays in which the main protagonist was some collective, usually fighting for its rights, were very fashionable. Yet what collective can we name as hero of *R.U.R.?* The play has no heroes. Robots and the six leading figures of Rossum's enterprise can hardly be called a collective. Instead, Čapek wanted to speak about the fate of mankind—

thus, about the greatest imaginable collective, and he designated the play accordingly.

At a time when the world's dramatists were the likes of Chekhov, Ibsen, and Strindberg, the contemporary stage depicted dramas of character and social struggle. Plays were full of passionate emotion, but Čapek had no interest in any of these aspects. He dismissed his love scenes with a few sentences parodying love scenes, and devoted most of his emphasis to deliberations about the results of mass production. A major part of the second act is devoted to his heroes' speculation as to their responsibility for the damage the Robots have caused mankind.

Čapek also dealt with dramatic time in a nontraditional manner. Ten years elapse between the prologue and first act (so that the actors' makeup had to be revised). An unspecified amount of time elapses between the second and third acts, but it has to be sufficient for the Robots to annihilate all of mankind. In the *Oresteia* of Aeschylus, between the murder of Agamemnon and the arrival of his son there is a lengthy interval of time during which the son grows to adulthood, without disturbing the unity of the drama. After all, the drama deals with acts of murder and revenge, not with the character of the murderer or avenger. In such a drama, after the death of the heroes there may still follow an epilogue, a reconciliation, an analysis of actions and their causes, in which new figures, new heroes, may appear. During an era when it was generally agreed that a drama was supposed to aim for a definite solution, Čapek followed the play's tragic climax and the murder of all the heroes with an additional act concerning the survival of intelligent life, as manifested by the Robots.

The play's language is worth noting. As the drama unfolds, the language becomes more pathetic and archaic—something especially surprising in connection with Čapek, who always endeavored to create a tongue as expressive as possible, and who truly succeeded in creating a new type of modern literary language derived from a masterfully grasped rhythm of spoken speech.

The names of Čapek's heroes are equally interesting. He sometimes chose names with a symbolic meaning (for example, in the novel *Krakatit* a man who symbolizes evil is called d'Henon, and late appears under the name Daimon), but he never used this approach as consistently as in *R.U.R.* The inventor of robots was old Rossum, while young Rossum adapted them for mass production as ideal workers with the least number of needs. (*Rossum* is related to the Czech word *Rozum*, meaning "reason.") The names of the two Rossums—who never actually appear in the play—thus symbolize reason as both creative and destructive. In Čapek's conception, it is reason that induces man to revolt against the traditional order, and in the end brings destruction to the whole race. Čapek derived the names of his characters from a variety of languages (he was fluent in five). Thus, Domin was clearly based on the Latin word *dominus*, master. Hallemeier has its origin in German—*Meier* is a manager and *Halle* a spacious hall or yard. Busman is short for *businessman*. Nana, who in the play represents a conservative feminine principle, is derived from the Russian word for nurse, and Dr. Gall from the famous Greek physician Galen. Čapek returned to this name once again, when he needed it for the pacifist physician who plays a leading role in the drama *The White Plague*. Fabry was clearly *homo faber*, man the creator. The architect Alquist is the one figure in the play who expresses most closely Čapek's own philosophy. His statements such as "I think it's better to lay a single brick than to draw up plans that are too great," and "there is nothing more terrible than giving people paradise on earth" echo repeatedly in Čapek's work. It is therefore appropriate that the name Alquist may be associated with the Latin *Aliquis* (somebody), as well as the Spanish *el quisto* (the favorite). The variety of the names' linguistic origins had a further symbolic value. It wasn't just isolated individuals who perished on the anonymous island; they were representatives of various nations—it was mankind that perished.

The second act, which Čapek explained as an apotheosis of the last people's heroism in their battle against hopeless odds, concerns above all a search for guilt. Who caused the catastrophe? Alquist cries: "I blame science! I blame technology! Domin! Myself! All of us! We, we are at fault!" Dr. Gall puts the blame on himself, for having tried to endow the Robots with a soul: "I am to blame for this. For everything that's happened." Helena similarly blames herself because she, too, tried to give Robots a soul. The other figures ponder the question of their guilt as well, although some excuse themselves by their faith in a utopian vision or blame forces beyond their control.

Čapek never strove for delicate character delineation, but in *R.U.R.* his figures lack any kind of psychological evolution. In fact, their actions are already prefigured by their names—each of them is a mere bearer of a single basic idea that he repeatedly proclaims. The deeds of the protagonists simply flow from their relation to a basic, fateful conflict between life and an unrealized utopia.

This returns the audience to the very beginnings of drama, to the great conflicts of fate in classical mythology. Čapek expressed his attraction for classical drama when he was a young man. In his critique of *Menaechmi* by Plautus, a comedy from the third century B.C., he praised the dramatic structure that later seemed to provide a guide to his Robot play.

> After all the emotional and moral peculiarities, after Ibsen, after the drama of the intimate . . . we came upon a simple, calm, direct antique comedy . . . From the very beginning, every figure has its one active interest, which in the course of the play is unequivocally pursued; there is no shift of will or changes of psychological development. The figures present themselves in a broad manner, they are meant to be typical, general and simple; their typicality gives them a maximum of life-like content, with a minimal need for characterizing detail and personal peculiarities. The dialogue proceeds by means of chronological explanation, and every idea is expressed by a monological, consistent explanation.

In classical drama, man is primarily a representative of his clan and as such leads a struggle for the meaning of his existence, for justice, truth, for the roots of his guilt. Conflict did not arise from the clash of characters but from the clash of principles or man's conflict with the higher powers of fate and supernatural forces, a clash that depended above all on the favor of disfavor of the gods.

In a mythical drama people do not only struggle with one another but also with a higher power of fate, with a judgment that man may combat, but cannot alter. It is important, however, that he succumb in a dignified manner. The destruction that in *R.U.R.* finally struck the representatives of humanity was not an expression of the will of gods, but the result of a human revolt against the laws of nature, against tradition, against human fate. Nevertheless, it was just as absolute, just as inescapable, just as fateful.

Even the pathos of some of the pronouncements seems to have found its inspiration in ancient drama, when pathos was still an essential part of fateful conflicts presented on stage. The names of the heroes, too, seem to symbolize the origin of Čapek's drama. In the course of millennia, the names of mythical heroes acquired symbolic values. Prometheus became a symbol of human revolt, Odysseus of intelligence that conquers force, Orpheus of a love that longs to overcome death. In the same way, Čapek's Domin was meant to be the symbol of a human being who wants "man to become a master! So he wouldn't have to live from hand to mouth!" Busman was a symbol of human submission to the marketplace and Alquist is Mister Somebody, one of us, who rejects the grandiose revolt and advises humility.

R.U.R. was a remarkable attempt to present to an atomized world a vision of mankind as a totality—to portray the destructive tendencies in man's behavior, to depict the basic discords in all their magnitude in a form simplified beyond the capabilities of realistic drama. To achieve this, it was necessary for individual figures to represent humanity, and to raise the forces they unleashed and by which they were overcome into fate itself. In capturing the fateful direction of the world's development, Čapek's message has lost none of its urgency.

When the thirty-one-year-old author witnessed the opening of *R.U.R.,* he had only eighteen years of life left to him. This short period coincided with the time left to the life of the prewar Czechoslovak Republic, connected above all with the name of President T. G. Masaryk. In the 1970s, the Czech dissident press held an opinion survey (unofficial, of course) as to the most significant personalities of modern Czech history. Karel Čapek was placed right behind President Masaryk. The two names truly belonged together. Čapek, younger than the president by two generations, became one of his closest friends and often served as his unofficial spokesman. From the early twenties onward the president would visit Čapek's villa to take part in the regular Friday meetings of Czech intellectuals. In his book *Talks with T. G. Masaryk,* Čapek presented a kind of compendium of the president's life experiences and his political, philosophical, and religious views. The book was a bestseller.

Čapek's entire life's work was performed within a span of some twenty years, testifying to the enormous depth of his talent. It is to his credit that after the world success of *R.U.R.* he didn't try to limit himself to an approach that brought him fame, but experimented in rapid succession with other literary genres, from travel books to modern fairy tales, to political essays, to detective stories. His work includes philosophical, witty discussions about art, mainly art on the margin of literature, such as detective stories, pornography, and popular urban poetry. (These writings have appeared in collected form, primarily in the book *In Praise of Newspapers.*) During the first World War, Čapek translated an extensive anthology of modern French poetry. This rare excursion into the poetic sphere provided extremely valuable inspiration for modern Czech poetry, as Czech poets continued to testify for several decades.

Customarily, Čapek's novels are considered the summit of his creation, be it the utopian novel *Krakatit* or the trilogy of novels dating from the early 1930s, *Hordubal, Meteor,* and *An Ordinary Life.* These are usually classed as philosophical prose, but in reality they are quite personal, and in spite of the exotic environment in which the first two novels are placed, these works have strongly autobiographical elements. Čapek's last utopian novel, *War with the Newts,* achieved an enthusiastic response. Here, returning to the basic idea of *R.U.R.,* Čapek describes a different type of intelligent being that revolts against humanity.

It is certainly true that these more extensive works may be considered weightier, philosophically and formally. *War with the Newts* has also become one of the wittiest polemics in world literature, as well as one of the sharpest satires on the politics of appeasement and the superficiality of our consumer civilization. As early as 1935, it predicted the catastrophic consequences of such developments.

Nevertheless, Čapek's extraordinary talent may have manifested itself most clearly in his short prose pieces and his feuilletons, written mainly for the newspaper *Lidové noviny*. Here he dealt with the daily concerns of average people, their pleasures, superstitions, loves, and encounters with the objects surrounding them. In his brief prose stories and columns he amazed his readers with his magnitude of witty insights and his encyclopedic knowledge, as well as with his ability to find something interesting, paradoxical, or stimulating in such everyday objects as a doorknob, a box of matches, a stove, or a vacuum cleaner.

These columns were collected in a series of books, including *The Gardener's Years, I Had a Dog and a Cat, Intimate Things, How a Play Is Produced,* and *Dashenka, or The Life of a Puppy.* Two volumes of Čapek's mystery stories, *Tales from Two Pockets,* gained extraordinary reader popularity.

Čapek also created his own genre of short prose, which he called "apocrypha." In a highly original, often humorous form, he reworked historical episodes or biblical events, or threw unexpected light upon mythical or literary figures.

In his last years, Čapek devoted a considerable part of his work to the struggle that took place in Europe between democracy and totalitarian systems. He wrote outstanding political essays, dealing above all with the responsibilities of the intelligentsia in totalitarian countries, as well as their ultimate treason. Čapek wrote two plays on current themes: *The White Plague* and *The Mother,* which involved intriguing and original themes, but suffered from a certain one-sidedness derived from the tense political situation. (However, at the time they attracted considerable public interest.) During this period, Čapek was ranked among the foremost European artists struggling to halt the expansion of German National Socialism.

In autumn 1938, after the disgraceful Munich agreement between Hitler and Western democratic powers, as a representative of the Masaryk concept of democracy Čapek became the target of attacks by ultra-rightists and the tabloid press. He stepped somewhat aside, doubtless depressed by the onslaught of totalitarian powers against which he had fought all his life. His outstanding last novel, *The Cheat,* in which he prophetically portrayed a man whose mediocrity and lack of creative talent, combined with a thirst for fame, made him a perfect symbol for the antihero of the oncoming age.

When it became evident that Hitler's occupation of Czechoslovakia was impending, Čapek's friends advised him to emigrate. There is no doubt that the door to other countries was open to him, especially in England, where he enjoyed a popularity matched by few foreign authors. However, Čapek refused to emigrate, wanting to remain with his threatened homeland and its people. On Christmas Day 1938 he fell ill, and a normally trivial respiratory illness became fatal. He died of pneumonia, a disease that only a few years later would have been treatable. He didn't live to see the war that fully confirmed his darkest forebodings. Perhaps that was fortunate because he was considered by the Nazis to be one of their foremost enemies. Most likely he would have perished in one of their concentration camps, a fate that befell many Czech intellectuals, including his brother Josef.

As was foretold by the unique response to *R.U.R.,* Čapek became the most famous of contemporary Czech writers, both at home and abroad. His work has been translated into numerous languages and, after almost a century, it is still being published anew. It still lives.

TRANSLATED BY PETER KUSSI

R.U.R.

(Rossum's Universal Robots)

*A Collective Drama in Three Acts
with a Comic Prologue*

CHARACTERS

HARRY DOMIN, central director of Rossum's Universal Robots

FABRY, engineer, general technical director of R.U.R.

DR. GALL, head of the physiological and research divisions of R.U.R.

DR. HALLEMEIER, head of the institute for Robot psychology and education

BUSMAN, general marketing director and chief counsel of R.U.R.

ALQUIST, builder, chief of construction of R.U.R.

HELENA GLORY

NANA, her nurse

MARIUS, a Robot

SULLA, a female Robot

RADIUS, a Robot

DAMON, a Robot

FIRST ROBOT

SECOND ROBOT

THIRD ROBOT

FOURTH ROBOT

ROBOT PRIMUS

ROBOT HELENA

ROBOT SERVANT and numerous other Robots

DOMIN, about thirty-eight years old in the Prologue, tall, clean-shaven

FABRY, also clean-shaven, fair-haired, with a serious and gentle face

DR. GALL, trifling, vivacious, suntanned, with a black mustache

HALLEMEIER, huge, robust, with a red, English mustache and red scrubby hair

BUSMAN, fat, bald, nearsighted

ALQUIST, older than the rest, carelessly dressed, with long, grizzled hair and whiskers

HELENA, very elegant

In the play proper everyone is ten years older than in the Prologue. In the Prologue the ROBOTS are dressed like people. Their movements and speech are laconic. Their faces are expressionless and their eyes fixed. In the play proper they are wearing linen shirts tightened at their waists with belts and have brass numbers on their chests. There are intermissions following the Prologue and the second act.

PROLOGUE

The central office of the Rossum's Universal Robots factory. On the right is a door. Windows in the front wall look out onto an endless row of factory buildings. On the left are more managerial offices.

DOMIN is sitting at a large American desk in a revolving armchair. On the desk are a lamp, a telephone, a paperweight, a file of letters, etc.; on the wall to the left are big maps depicting ship and railway lines, a big calendar, and a clock that reads shortly before noon; affixed to the wall on the left are printed posters: "The Cheapest Labor: Rossum's Robots." "New—Tropical Robots— $150." "Buy Your Very Own Robot." "Looking to Cut Production Costs? Order Rossum's Robots." Yet more maps, transport regulations, a table of telegraph rates, etc. In contrast to these wall decorations there is a splendid Turkish carpet on the floor, and to the right are a round table, a couch, a leather club-style armchair, and a bookcase containing bottles of wine and brandy instead of books. On the left is a safe. Next to DOMIN's desk is a typewriter at which SULLA is working.

DOMIN [*dictating*]: "—that we will not stand responsible for goods damaged in transport. Just before loading we brought it to the attention of your captain that the ship was unfit for the transportation of Robots, so we cannot be held financially accountable for any damage to the merchandise. For Rossum's Universal Robots, etcetera—" Got it?

SULLA: Yes.

DOMIN: Next letter. Friedrichswerke, Hamburg.—Date.— "I am writing to confirm your order for fifteen thousand Robots—" [*In-house telephone rings. DOMIN answers it.*]

Hello—Central office here—Yes.—Certainly. But of course, as usual.—Of course, wire them.—Good.—[*He hangs up the telephone.*] Where did I leave off?

SULLA: "I am writing to confirm your order for fifteen thousand Robots."

DOMIN [*thinking*]: Fifteen thousand Robots. Fifteen thousand Robots.

MARIUS [*enters*]: Mr. Director, a lady is asking—

DOMIN: Who is it?

MARIUS: I do not know. [*He hands* DOMIN *a calling card.*]

DOMIN [*reads*]: President Glory.—Ask her in.

MARIUS [*opens the door*]: If you please, ma'am.

[HELENA GLORY *enters.* MARIUS *leaves.*]

DOMIN [*stands*]: How do you do?

HELENA: Central Director Domin?

DOMIN: At your service.

HELENA: I have come—

DOMIN: —with a note from President Glory. That's fine.

HELENA: President Glory is my father. I am Helena Glory.

DOMIN: Miss Glory, it is an unusual honor for us to . . . to . . .

HELENA: To be unable to show you the door?

DOMIN: To welcome the daughter of our great president. Please have a seat. Sulla, you may go.

[SULLA *leaves.*]

DOMIN [*sits down*]: How can I be of service, Miss Glory?

HELENA: I have come—

DOMIN: —to have a look at our factory production of people. Like all our visitors. I'd be happy to show you.

HELENA: But I thought it was prohibited—

DOMIN: —to enter the factory, of course. Yet everyone comes here with someone's calling card, Miss Glory.

HELENA: And you show everyone . . . ?

DOMIN: Only some things. The production of artificial people is a factory secret, Miss Glory.

HELENA: If you knew just how much—

DOMIN: —this interests you. Good old Europe is talking about nothing else.

HELENA: Why don't you let me finish my sentences?

DOMIN: I beg your pardon. Perhaps you wanted to say something different?

HELENA: I only wanted to ask—

DOMIN: —whether I wouldn't make an exception and show you our factory. But of course, Miss Glory.

HELENA: How did you know that's what I wanted to ask?

DOMIN: Everyone asks the same thing. [*He stands.*] With all due respect, Miss Glory, we will show you more than we show the others, and—in a word—

HELENA: I thank you.

DOMIN: If you swear that you will not disclose to anyone even the smallest—

HELENA [*stands and offers him her hand*]: You have my word of honor.

DOMIN: Thank you. Don't you want to take off your veil?

HELENA: Oh, of course, you want to see . . . Excuse me.

DOMIN: Pardon?

HELENA: If you would let go of my hand.

DOMIN [*lets go of her hand*]: I beg your pardon.

HELENA [*taking off her veil*]: You want to see that I'm not a spy. How cautious you are.

DOMIN [*scrutinizing her ardently*]: Hmm, of course, we—yes.

HELENA: Don't you trust me?

DOMIN: Absolutely, Hele—pardon, Miss Glory. Really, I'm extraordinarily delighted. Did you have a good crossing?

HELENA: Yes. Why?

DOMIN: Because I was just thinking—you're still very young.

HELENA: Will we be going to the factory immediately?

DOMIN: Yes. I'd guess about twenty-two, right?

HELENA: Twenty-two what?

DOMIN: Years old.

HELENA: Twenty-one. Why do you want to know?

DOMIN: Because—since—[*Enthusiastically.*] You'll stay awhile, won't you?

HELENA: That depends on what I see at the factory.

DOMIN: Damned factory! But certainly, Miss Glory, you will see everything. Please, have a seat. Would you be interested in learning something about the history of the invention?

HELENA: Yes, please. [*She sits down.*]

DOMIN: Well, then. [*He sits down at the desk, gazing rapturously at Helena, and rattles off quickly.*] The year was 1920 when old Rossum, a great philosopher but at the time still a young scholar, moved away to this remote island to study marine life, period. At the same time he was attempting to reproduce, by means of chemical synthesis, living matter known as protoplasm, when suddenly he discovered a substance that behaved exactly like living matter although it was of a different chemical composition. That was in 1932, precisely four hundred forty years after the discovery of America.

HELENA: You know all this by heart?

DOMIN: Yes. Physiology, Miss Glory, is not my long suit. Shall I go on?

HELENA: Please.

DOMIN [*solemnly*]: And then, Miss Glory, among his chemical formulae, old Rossum wrote "Nature has found only one process by which to organize living matter. There is, however, another process, simpler, more moldable and faster, that nature has not hit upon at all. It is this other process, by means of which the development of life could proceed, that I have discovered this very day." Imagine, Miss Glory, that he wrote these lofty words about some phlegm of a colloidal jelly that not even a dog would eat. Imagine him sitting over a test tube and thinking how the whole tree of life would grow out of it, starting with some species of worm and ending—ending with man himself. Man made from a different matter than we are. Miss Glory, that was a tremendous moment.

HELENA: What then?

DOMIN: Then? Then it was a question of taking life out of the test tube, speeding up its development, shaping some of the organs, bones, nerves, and whatnot, and finding certain substances, catalysts, enzymes, hormones, etcetera; in short, do you understand?

HELENA: I d-d-don't know. Not very much, I'm afraid.

DOMIN: I don't get it at all. Anyway with the help of these potions he could make whatever he wanted. For instance, he could have created a jellyfish with a Socratic brain or a one-hundred-fifty-foot worm. But because he hadn't a shred of humor about him, he took it into his head to create an ordinary vertebrate, possibly a human being. And so he set to it.

HELENA: To what?

DOMIN: To reproducing nature. First he tried to create an artificial dog. That took him a number of years, and finally he produced something like a mutant calf that died in a couple of days. I'll point it out to you in the museum. And then old Rossum set out to manufacture a human being.

[*Pause*]

HELENA: And *this* is what I shouldn't tell anyone?

DOMIN: No one in the world.

HELENA: It's a pity this is already in all the papers.

DOMIN: A pity. [*He jumps up from the desk and sits down next to Helena.*] But do you know what isn't in the papers? [*He taps his forehead.*] That old Rossum was a raving lunatic. That's a fact, Miss Glory, but keep it to yourself. That old eccentric actually wanted to make *people*.

HELENA: But you *do* make people!

DOMIN: More or less, Miss Glory. But old Rossum meant that literally. You see, he wanted to somehow scientifically dethrone God. He was a frightful materialist and did everything on that account. For him the question was just to prove that God is unnecessary. So he resolved to create a human being just like us, down to the last hair. Do you know a little anatomy?

HELENA: Only—very little.

DOMIN: Same here. Imagine, he took it into his head to manufacture everything just as it is in the human body, right down to the last gland. The appendix, the tonsils, the belly button—all the superfluities. Finally even—hmm—even the sexual organs.

HELENA: But after all those—those after all . . .

DOMIN: Are not superfluous, I know. But if people were going to be produced artificially, then it was not—hmm—in any way necessary—

HELENA: I understand.

DOMIN: I'll show you in the museum what all he managed to bungle in ten years. The thing that was supposed to be a man lived for three whole days. Old Rossum had no taste. What he did was dreadful. But inside, that thing had all the stuff a person has. Actually, it was amazingly detailed work. And then young Rossum, an engineer, the son of the old man, came here. An ingenious mind, Miss Glory. When he saw what a scene his old man was making he said: "This is non-sense! Ten years to produce a human being?! If you can't do it faster than nature then what's the point?" And he launched into anatomy himself.

HELENA: It's different in the papers.

DOMIN [stands]: The papers are full of paid ads; all the rest is nonsense. They say, for example, that the old man invented the Robots. The fact is that the old man was well suited to the university, but he had no sense of factory production. He thought he would make real people, possibly a new race of Indians, be they professors or idiots, you see? It was young Rossum who had the idea to create living and intelligent la-bor machines from this mess. All that stuff in the papers about the collaboration of the two great Rossums is a fairy tale. Those two quarreled brutally. The old atheist didn't have a crumb of understanding for industry, and finally young Rossum shut him up in some laboratory where he could fid-dle with his monumental abortions, and he himself under-took production from the standpoint of an engineer. Old Rossum literally cursed him, and before his death he bungled two more physiological monsters until he was finally found dead in his laboratory one day. That's the whole story.

HELENA: And what about the young man?

DOMIN: Young Rossum was of a new age, Miss Glory. The age of production following the age of discovery. When he took a look at human anatomy he saw immediately that it was too complex and that a good engineer could simplify it. So he undertook to redesign anatomy, experimenting with what would lend itself to omission or simplification . . . In short, Miss Glory—but isn't this boring you?

HELENA: No, on the contrary, it's terribly interesting.

DOMIN: So then young Rossum said to himself: A human being. That's something that feels joy, plays the violin, wants to go for a walk, in general requires a lot of things that—that are, in effect, superfluous.

HELENA: Oh!

DOMIN: Wait. That are superfluous when he needs to weave, say, or add. A gasoline engine doesn't need tassels and ornaments, Miss Glory. And manufacturing artificial workers is exactly like manufacturing gasoline engines. Production should be as simple as possible, and the product the best for its function. What do you think? From a practical standpoint, what is the best kind of worker?

HELENA: The best? Probably one who—who—who is honest—and dedicated.

DOMIN: No, it's the one that's the cheapest. The one with the fewest needs. Young Rossum successfully invented a worker with the smallest number of needs, but to do so he had to simplify him. He chucked everything not directly related to work, and in so doing he pretty much discarded the human being and created the Robot. My dear Miss Glory, Robots are not people. They are mechanically more perfect than we are, they have an astounding intellectual capacity, but they have no soul. Oh, Miss Glory, the creation of an engineer is technically more refined than the product of nature.

HELENA: It is said that man is the creation of God.

DOMIN: So much the worse. God had no grasp of modern technology. Would you believe that the late young Rossum assumed the role of God?

HELENA: How, may I ask?

DOMIN: He started manufacturing Superrobots. Working giants. He experimented with making them twelve feet tall, but you wouldn't believe how those mammoths kept falling apart.

HELENA: Falling apart?

DOMIN: Yes. All of a sudden for no reason a leg would break or something. Our planet is apparently too small for giants. Now we make only Robots of normal human height and respectable human shape.

HELENA: I saw the first Robots back home. The township bought them . . . I mean hired—

DOMIN: Bought, my dear Miss Glory. Robots are bought.

HELENA: We acquired them, as street-cleaners. I've seen them sweeping. They are so strange, so quiet.

DOMIN: Have you seen my secretary?

HELENA: I didn't notice.

DOMIN [*rings*]: You see, the Rossum's Universal Robots Corporation does not yet manufacture entirely uniform goods. Some of the Robots are very fine, others come out cruder. The best will live perhaps twenty years.

HELENA: Then they die?

DOMIN: Well, they wear out.

[*Enter* SULLA.]

DOMIN: Sulla, let Miss Glory have a look at you.

HELENA [*stands and offers* SULLA *her hand*]: How do you do? You must be dreadfully sad out here so far away from the rest of the world, no?

SULLA: That I cannot say, Miss Glory. Please have a seat.

HELENA [*sits down*]: Where are you from, Miss?

SULLA: From here, from the factory.

HELENA: Oh, you were born here?

SULLA: I was made here, yes.

HELENA [*jumping up*]: What?

DOMIN [*laughing*]: Sulla is not human, Miss Glory. Sulla is a Robot.

HELENA: I beg your pardon . . .

DOMIN [*placing his hand on* SULLA's *shoulder*]: Sulla's not offended. Take a look at the complexion we make, Miss Glory. Touch her face.

HELENA: Oh, no, no!

DOMIN: You'd never guess she was made from a different substance than we are. She even has the characteristic soft hair of a blonde, if you please. Only the eyes are a bit . . . But on the other hand, what hair! Turn around, Sulla!

HELENA: Please stop!

DOMIN: Chat with our guest, Sulla. She is a distinguished visitor.

SULLA: Please, Miss, have a seat. [*They both sit down.*] Did you have a good crossing?

HELENA: Yes—cer-certainly.

SULLA: Do not go back on the *Amelia,* Miss Glory. The barometer is falling sharply—to 705 torr. Wait for the *Pennsylvania*; it is a very good, very strong ship.

DOMIN: Speed?

SULLA: Twenty knots. Tonnage—twenty thousand.

DOMIN [*laughing*]: Enough, Sulla, enough. Let's hear how well you speak French.

HELENA: You know French?

SULLA: I know four languages. I can write, "Ctěný pane! Monsieur! Geehrter Herr! Dear Sir!"

HELENA [*jumping up*]: This is preposterous! You are a charlatan! Sulla's not a Robot, Sulla is a young woman just like me! Sulla, this is disgraceful—why do you play along with this farce?

SULLA: I am a Robot.

HELENA: No, no, you are lying! Oh, Sulla, forgive me, I understand—they've forced you to act as a living advertisement for them! Sulla, you are a young woman like me, aren't you? Tell me you are!

DOMIN: I'm sorry to disappoint you, Miss Glory. Sulla is a Robot.

HELENA: You're lying!

DOMIN [*drawing himself up*]: What?! [*He rings.*] Excuse me, Miss Glory, but I must convince you.

[*Enter* MARIUS.]

DOMIN: Marius, take Sulla into the dissecting room so they can open her up. Quickly!

HELENA: Where?

DOMIN: The dissecting room. When they have cut her open you can go and take a look at her.

HELENA: I won't go.

DOMIN: Excuse me, but you accused me of lying.

HELENA: You want to have her killed?

DOMIN: Machines cannot be killed.

HELENA [*embracing* SULLA]: Don't be frightened, Sulla. I

won't let them hurt you! Tell me, darling, is everyone so in-
humane to you? You mustn't put up with that, do you hear?
You mustn't, Sulla!

SULLA: I am a Robot.

HELENA: That makes no difference. Robots are every bit as
good people as we are. Sulla, you'd let them cut you open?

SULLA: Yes.

HELENA: Oh, you are not afraid of death?

SULLA: I am not familiar with it, Miss Glory.

HELENA: Do you know what would happen to you then?

SULLA: Yes, I would stop moving.

HELENA: This is d-r-readful!

DOMIN: Marius, tell Miss Glory what you are.

MARIUS: Robot Marius.

DOMIN: Would you put Sulla in the dissecting room?

MARIUS: Yes.

DOMIN: Would you be sorry for her?

MARIUS: I do not know "sorry."

DOMIN: What would happen to her?

MARIUS: She would stop moving. She would be sent to the
stamping-mill.

DOMIN: That is death, Marius. Do you fear death?

MARIUS: No.

DOMIN: So you see, Miss Glory. Robots do not cling to life.
They can't. They don't have the means—no soul, no pleasures. Grass has more will to live than they do.

HELENA: Oh, stop! At least send them out of the room!

DOMIN: Marius, Sulla, you may go.

[SULLA *and* MARIUS *leave.*]

HELENA: They are d-r-readful! What you are doing is abominable!

DOMIN: Why abominable?

HELENA: I don't know. Why—why did you name her Sulla?

DOMIN: You don't think it's a pretty name?

HELENA: It's a man's name. Sulla was a Roman general.

DOMIN: Oh, we thought that Marius and Sulla were lovers.

HELENA: No, Marius and Sulla were generals and fought
against each other in the year—the year—I don't remember
anymore.

DOMIN: Come over to the window. What do you see?

HELENA: Bricklayers.

DOMIN: Those are Robots. All our laborers are Robots. And down below, can you see anything?

HELENA: Some sort of office.

DOMIN: The accounting office. And its . . .

HELENA: . . . full of office workers.

DOMIN: Robots. All our office staff are Robots. When you see the factory . . .

[*At that moment the factory whistles and sirens sound.*]

DOMIN: Noon. The Robots don't know when to stop working. At two o'clock I'll show you the kneading troughs.

HELENA: What kneading troughs?

DOMIN [*drily*]: The mixing vats for the batter. In each one we mix enough batter to make a thousand Robots at a time. Then there are the vats for livers, brains, etcetera. Then you'll see the bone factory, and after that I'll show you the spinning mill.

HELENA: What spinning mill?

DOMIN: The spinning mill for nerves. The spinning mill for veins. The spinning mill where miles and miles of digestive tract are made at once. Then there's the assembly plant, where all of this is put together, you know, like automobiles. Each worker is responsible for affixing one part, and then it automatically moves on to a second worker, then to a third, and so on. It's a most fascinating spectacle. Next comes the drying kiln and the stock room, where the brand new products are put to work.

HELENA: Good heavens, they have to work immediately?

DOMIN: Sorry. They work the same way new furniture works. They get broken in. Somehow they heal up internally or something. Even a lot that's new grows up inside them. You understand, we have to leave a bit of room for natural development. And in the meantime the products are refined.

HELENA: How do you mean?

DOMIN: Well, it's the same as "school" for people. They learn to speak, write, and do calculations. They have a phenomenal memory. If you were to read them a twenty-volume encyclopedia they could repeat the contents in order, but they never think up anything original. They'd make fine university professors. Next they are sorted by grade and distributed. Fifty thousand head a day, not counting the inevitable percentage of defective ones that are thrown into the stamping-mill . . . etcetera, etcetera.

HELENA: Are you angry with me?

DOMIN: God forbid! I only thought that . . . that perhaps we could talk about other things. We are only a handful of people here amidst a hundred thousand Robots, and there are no women. It's as though we're cursed, Miss Glory.

HELENA: I'm so sorry that I said that—that—that you were lying—

[*A knock at the door.*]

DOMIN: Come in, boys.

[DR. GALL, DR. HALLEMEIER, *the engineer* FABRY, *and the builder* ALQUIST *enter from the left.*]

DR. GALL: Excuse us, I hope we're not interrupting?

DOMIN: Come here. Miss Glory, let me introduce Alquist, Fabry, Gall, and Hallemeier. The daughter of President Glory.

HELENA [*at a loss*]: Hello.

FABRY: We had no idea—

DR. GALL: We are deeply honored—

ALQUIST: Welcome, Miss Glory.

[BUSMAN *rushes in from the right.*]

BUSMAN: Hey, what have we here?

DOMIN: Here, Busman. This is our Busman, Miss. [*To* BUSMAN.] The daughter of President Glory.

HELENA: How do you do?

BUSMAN: Why, this is splendid! Miss Glory, shall we wire the papers that you have done us the honor to pay a visit—?

HELENA: No, no, I beg you!

DOMIN: Please, Miss Glory, have a seat.

FABRY ⎫   Excuse us—
BUSMAN ⎬ [*drawing up easy chairs*]: Please—
DR. GALL ⎭   Pardon—

ALQUIST: Miss Glory, how was your trip?

DR. GALL: Will you be staying with us long?

FABRY: What do you have to say about the factory, Miss Glory?

HALLEMEIER: Did you come on the *Amelia*?

DOMIN: Quiet, let Miss Glory speak.

HELENA [*to* DOMIN]: What should I talk to them about?

DOMIN [*with astonishment*]: Whatever you want.

HELENA: Should I . . . may I speak quite openly?

DOMIN: But of course.

HELENA [*hesitates, then is desperately determined*]: Tell me, isn't the way they treat you here hurtful sometimes?

FABRY: Who, may I ask?

HELENA: All the people.
[*They all look at each other, puzzled.*]

ALQUIST: Treat us?

DR. GALL: Why do you think that?

HALLEMEIER: Thunderation!

BUSMAN: God forbid, Miss Glory!

HELENA: I'm sure you must feel that you could have a better existence?

DR. GALL: That depends, Miss Glory. How do you mean that?

HELENA: I mean that—[*She explodes.*]—this is abominable! This is awful! [*She stands up.*] All of Europe is talking about what's happening to you here! So I came here to see for myself, and it's a thousand times worse than anyone ever imagined! How can you stand it?

ALQUIST: Stand what?

HELENA: Your position. For God's sake, you are people just like us, like all of Europe, like the whole world! The way you live is undignified, it's scandalous!

BUSMAN: Dear Lord, Miss!

FABRY: No, boys, she's right in a way. We really do live like savages here.

HELENA: Worse than savages! May I, oh, may I call you brothers?

BUSMAN: But good Lord, why not?

HELENA: Brothers, I have not come as the president's daughter. I have come on behalf of the League of Humanity. Brothers, the League of Humanity already has more than two hundred

thousand members. Two hundred thousand people stand behind you and offer you their support.

BUSMAN: Two hundred thousand people! That's quite respectable, that's beautiful.

FABRY: It's like I'm always saying: nothing beats good old Europe. You see, they haven't forgotten about us. They're offering us help.

DR. GALL: What kind of help? A theater?

HALLEMEIER: A symphony orchestra?

HELENA: More than that.

ALQUIST: You yourself?

HELENA: Oh, that goes without saying. I'll stay as long as I am
needed.

BUSMAN: God in heaven, this is joy!

ALQUIST: Domin, I'll go and get our best room ready for Miss
Glory.

DOMIN: Wait just a minute. I'm afraid that—that Miss Glory
has not yet said everything she has to say.

HELENA: No, I have not. Unless you plan to shut my mouth by
force.

DR. GALL: Just you try it, Harry!

HELENA: Thank you. I knew you would stand up for me.

DOMIN: Excuse me, Miss Glory. Do you think that you're talking to Robots?

HELENA [*pauses*]: Of course, what else?

DOMIN: I'm sorry. These gentlemen are people, just like you.
Like all of Europe.

HELENA [*to the others*]: You're not Robots?

BUSMAN [*guffawing*]: God forbid!

HALLEMEIER: Bah, Robots!

DR. GALL [*laughing*]: Thank you very much!

HELENA: But . . . this is impossible!

FABRY: On my honor, Miss Glory, we are not Robots.

HELENA [*to* DOMIN]: Then why did you tell me that all of your
office staff are Robots?

DOMIN: The office staff, yes, but not the directors. Miss Glory,
allow me to introduce Fabry, general technical director of
Rossum's Universal Robots; Doctor Gall, head of the physiological and research divisions; Doctor Hallemeier, head of

the institute of Robot psychology and education; Busman, general marketing director and chief counsel; and our builder Alquist, chief of construction at Rossum's Universal Robots.

HELENA: Forgive me, gentlemen, for—for— Is what I have done d-r-readful?

ALQUIST: Good heavens, Miss Glory. Please, have a seat.

HELENA [*sits down*]: I'm a silly girl. Now—now you'll send me back on the first boat.

DR. GALL: Not for anything in the world, Miss Glory. Why would we send you away?

HELENA: Because now you know—because—because I came to incite the Robots.

DOMIN: Dear Miss Glory, we've already had at least a hundred saviors and prophets here. Every boat brings another one. Missionaries, anarchists, the Salvation Army, everything imaginable. It would amaze you to know how many churches and lunatics there are in the world.

HELENA: And you let them talk to the Robots?

DOMIN: Why not? So far they've all given up. The Robots remember everything, but nothing more. They don't even laugh at what people say. Actually, it's hard to believe. If it would interest you, dear Miss Glory, I'll take you to the Robot warehouse. There are about three hundred thousand of them there.

BUSMAN: Three hundred forty-seven thousand.

DOMIN: Good. You can tell them whatever you want. You can read them the Bible, logarithms, or whatever you please. You can even preach to them about human rights.

HELENA: Oh, I thought that . . . if someone were to show them a bit of love—

FABRY: Impossible, Miss Glory. Nothing is farther from being human than a Robot.

HELENA: Why do you make them then?

BUSMAN: Hahaha, that's a good one! Why do we make Robots!

FABRY: For work, Miss. One Robot can do the work of two and a half human laborers. The human machine, Miss Glory, was hopelessly imperfect. It needed to be done away with once and for all.

BUSMAN: It was too costly.

FABRY: It was less than efficient. It couldn't keep up with modern technology. And secondly, it's great progress that . . . pardon.

HELENA: What?

FABRY: Forgive me. It's great progress to give birth by machine. It's faster and more convenient. Any acceleration constitutes progress, Miss Glory. Nature had no grasp of the modern rate of work. From a technical standpoint the whole of childhood is pure nonsense. Simply wasted time. An untenable waste of time. And thirdly . . .

HELENA: Oh, stop!

FABRY: I'm sorry. Let me ask you, what exactly does this League of—League of—League of Humanity of yours want?

HELENA: We want first and foremost to protect the Robots and—and—to guarantee them—good treatment.

FABRY: That's not a bad goal. Machines should be treated well. Honestly, that makes me happy. I don't like damaged goods. Please, Miss Glory, enlist us all as contributing, dues-paying, founding members of your League!

HELENA: No, you misunderstand me. We want . . . specifically . . . we want to liberate the Robots.

HALLEMEIER: How, may I ask?

HELENA: They should be treated like . . . treated like . . . like people.

HALLEMEIER: Aha. Perhaps they should be allowed to vote, too? You won't go so far as to say that they should be paid?

HELENA: But of course they should!

HALLEMEIER: Let's think about this. If they had money, what would they do with it?

HELENA: Buy themselves . . . what they need . . . whatever would make them happy.

HALLEMEIER: That's very nice, Miss, but nothing makes Robots happy. Dear God, what would they buy for themselves? You can feed them pineapples or straw or whatever—it's all the same to them. They have no sense of taste. They have no interest in anything, Miss Glory. By God, no one's ever even seen a Robot smile.

HELENA: Why . . . why . . . why don't you make them happier?

HALLEMEIER: It's no use, Miss Glory. They're only Robots. They have no will of their own, no passion, no history, no soul.

HELENA: No love or defiance, either?

HALLEMEIER: That goes without saying. Robots love nothing, not even themselves. And defiance? I don't know; only rarely, every once in a while . . .

HELENA: What?

HALLEMEIER: Nothing special. Occasionally they go crazy somehow. Something like epilepsy, you know? We call it Robotic Palsy. All of a sudden one of them goes and breaks whatever it has in its hand, stops working, gnashes its teeth—and we have to send it to the stamping mill. Evidently a breakdown of the organism.

DOMIN: A flaw in production.

HELENA: No, no, that's a soul!

FABRY: You think that a soul begins with the gnashing of teeth?

DOMIN: We'll soon put a stop to all of this, Miss Glory. Doctor Gall is doing some significant experiments . . .

DR. GALL: Not on that, Domin; right now I'm making pain-reactive nerves.

HELENA: Pain-reactive nerves?

DR. GALL: Yes. Robots feel almost no physical pain. You see, the late young Rossum oversimplified the nervous system. That was no good. We must introduce suffering.

HELENA: Why—why—If you won't give them souls, why do you want to give them pain?

DR. GALL: For industrial reasons, Miss Glory. The Robots sometimes damage themselves because nothing hurts them. They stick their hands into machines, break their fingers, smash their heads, it's all the same to them. We must give them pain; it's a built-in safeguard against damage.

HELENA: Will they be happier when they can feel pain?

DR. GALL: On the contrary. But they will be technically more perfect.

HELENA: Why won't you make souls for them?

DR. GALL: That's not within our power.

FABRY: Nor in our interest.

BUSMAN: That would raise the cost of production. Dear Lord, lovely lady, the beauty of our product is that it's so cheap! One hundred twenty dollars a head, complete with clothing, and fifteen years ago they cost ten thousand. Five years ago we were still buying clothes for them. Today we have our own textile mill where we produce fabric five times more cheaply than other factories. Tell me, Miss Glory, what do you pay for a bolt of cloth?

HELENA: I don't know . . . actually . . . I've forgotten.

BUSMAN: Good Lord, and you want to found a League of Humanity! Ours costs only a third as much, Miss Glory; today all prices are only a third of what they were, and they're still falling, falling, falling—just like that. Well?

HELENA: I don't understand.

BUSMAN: Lord, Miss Glory. What this means is that we've cut the cost of labor. Why, even with fodder a Robot costs only three-quarters of a cent an hour. It's really funny, Miss, how factories all over are going belly-up unless they've bought Robots to cut production costs.

HELENA: Yes, and human workers are getting sacked.

BUSMAN: Haha, that goes without saying. But in the meantime we've dropped five hundred thousand tropical Robots on the Argentine pampas to tend the wheat. Tell me, please, what do you pay for a loaf of bread?

HELENA: I have no idea.

BUSMAN: Well, you see, right now bread costs two cents a loaf in your good old Europe; that's the daily bread *we* can provide, do you understand? Two cents for a loaf of bread and your League of Humanity knows nothing about it! Haha, Miss Glory, what you don't know is that even *that* is too expensive per slice. For the sake of civilization, etcetera. What would you bet that in five years—

HELENA: What?

BUSMAN: In five years everything will cost a tenth of what it costs now. Folks, in five years we'll be drowning in wheat and everything else you could possibly want.

ALQUIST: Yes, and all the laborers of the world will be out of work.

DOMIN [*stands up*]: Yes they will, Alquist. They will, Miss

Glory. But within the next ten years Rossum's Universal Robots will produce so much wheat, so much cloth, so much everything that things will no longer have any value. Everyone will be able to take as much as he needs. There'll be no more poverty. Yes, people will be out of work, but by then there'll be no work left to be done. Everything will be done by living machines. People will do only what they enjoy. They will live only to perfect themselves.

HELENA [*stands*]: Will it really be so?

DOMIN: It will. It can't be otherwise. But before that some awful things may happen, Miss Glory. That just can't be avoided. But then the subjugation of man by man and the enslavement of man by matter will cease. Never again will anyone pay for his bread with hatred and his life. There'll be no more laborers, no more secretaries. No one will have to mine coal or slave over someone else's machines. No longer will man need to destroy his soul doing work that he hates.

ALQUIST: Domin, Domin! What you're saying sounds too much like paradise. Domin, there was something good in the act of serving, something great in humility. Oh, Harry, there was some kind of virtue in work and fatigue.

DOMIN: There probably was. But we can't exactly compensate for everything that's lost when we recreate the world from Adam. O Adam, Adam! no longer will you have to earn your bread by the sweat of your brow; you will return to Paradise, where you were nourished by the hand of God. You will be free and supreme; you will have no other task, no other work, no other cares than to perfect your own being. You will be the master of creation.

BUSMAN: Amen.

FABRY: Let it be.

HELENA: I'm thoroughly confused. I guess I'm just a silly girl. I'd like . . . I'd like to believe all this.

DR. GALL: You're younger than we are, Miss Glory. You'll live to see it all.

HALLEMEIER: Right. I think that Miss Glory might have lunch with us.

DR. GALL: Well, *that* goes without saying! Domin, why don't you offer the invitation on behalf of us all.

DOMIN: Miss Glory, do us this honor.

HELENA: But really . . . How could I?

FABRY: For the League of Humanity, Miss Glory.

BUSMAN: In its honor.

HELENA: Well, in that case . . . perhaps . . .

FABRY: Splendid! Miss Glory, excuse me for five minutes.

DR. GALL: Pardon.

BUSMAN: Good Lord, I must wire . . .

HALLEMEIER: Damn, I forgot . . .

[*Everyone except* DOMIN *rushes out.*]

HELENA: Why did they all leave?

DOMIN: To cook, Miss Glory.

HELENA: Cook what?

DOMIN: Lunch, Miss Glory. The Robots cook for *us,* but . . . but . . . because they have no sense of taste it's not quite . . . Hallemeier makes an outstanding roast. Gall can whip up such a gravy, and Busman's a whiz at omelets.

HELENA: Goodness, what a feast! And what about Mr. . . . the builder . . . What does he do?

DOMIN: Alquist? Nothing. He'll set the table, and—and Fabry will throw together a fruit salad. A very modest kitchen, Miss Glory.

HELENA: I wanted to ask you . . .

DOMIN: There's something I would like to ask you, too. [*He places his watch on the table.*] We have five minutes.

HELENA: What is it?

DOMIN: Sorry, you first.

HELENA: This may sound silly, but . . . Why do you manufacture female Robots, when . . . when . . .

DOMIN: When they, hmm, when sex means nothing to them?

HELENA: Exactly.

DOMIN: There's a certain demand, you see? Waitresses, shopgirls, secretaries—it's what people are used to.

HELENA: Then . . . then tell me, are the male Robots . . . and the female Robots simply . . . simply . . .

DOMIN: Simply indifferent to each other, dear Miss Glory. They don't exhibit even traces of attraction.

HELENA: Oh, that is d-r-readful!

DOMIN: Why?

HELENA: It's so . . . so . . . so unnatural! I don't know whether
to loathe them, or . . . envy them . . . or perhaps even . . .

DOMIN: Feel sorry for them?

HELENA: That most of all!—No, stop! You wanted to ask me
something?

DOMIN: I would like to ask, Miss Glory, whether you would
take me—

HELENA: Take you where?

DOMIN: As your husband.

HELENA: Absolutely not! What's gotten into you?

DOMIN [*looks at his watch*]: Three more minutes. If you won't
have me you must at least marry one of the other five.

HELENA: Oh, God forbid! Why would I marry one of them?

DOMIN: Because they'll all ask you.

HELENA: How could they dare?

DOMIN: I'm very sorry, Miss Glory. It appears that they've
fallen in love with you.

HELENA: Please, don't let them do this! I—I will leave immediately.

DOMIN: Helena, you don't have the heart to disappoint them
with a rejection?

HELENA: But—but I can't marry all six of you!

DOMIN: No, but at least one. If you don't want me then take
Fabry.

HELENA: I don't want him.

DOMIN: Doctor Gall then.

HELENA: No, no, be quiet! I don't want any of you!

DOMIN: Two more minutes.

HELENA: This is d-r-readful! Marry some female Robot.

DOMIN: A female Robot is not a woman.

HELENA: Oh, that's all you want! I think you—you'd marry
any woman who came along.

DOMIN: Others have been here, Helena.

HELENA: Young ones?

DOMIN: Young ones.

HELENA: Why didn't you marry any of them?

DOMIN: Because I've never lost my head. Until today. The moment you took off your veil.

HELENA: I know.

DOMIN: One more minute.

HELENA: But I don't want to, for God's sake!

DOMIN [*places his hands on her shoulders*]: One more minute. Either look me straight in the eye and say something terribly evil and I'll leave you alone, or else—or else—

HELENA: You're a brute!

DOMIN: That's nothing. A man should be a bit of a brute. That's in the natural order of things.

HELENA: You're a lunatic!

DOMIN: People should be a little loony, Helena. That's the best thing about them.

HELENA: You are—you are—oh, God!

DOMIN: There, you see? Ready?

HELENA: No! Please, let go of me. You're c-r-r-rushing me!

DOMIN: Last chance, Helena.

HELENA [*restraining herself*]: Not for anything in the world— But Harry! [*A knock at the door.*]

DOMIN [*lets go of her*]: Come in!

[*Enter* BUSMAN, DR. GALL, *and* HALLEMEIER *in chefs' aprons.* FABRY *is carrying flowers and* ALQUIST *has a tablecloth under his arm.*]

DOMIN: All set?

BUSMAN [*gaily*]: Yes.

DOMIN: So are we.

Curtain

ACT ONE

HELENA's *sitting room. To the left a wallpapered door leads into a music room. To the right is a door leading into* HELENA's *bedroom. In the center is a window looking out onto the sea and the docks. The room is furnished with a cosmetic mirror surrounded by toiletries and feminine trifles, a table, a sofa and armchair, a commode, and a small writing table with a floor lamp next to it. To the right is a fireplace with a floor lamp on either side. The entire sitting room, down to the last detail, has a modern and purely feminine look.*

   DOMIN, FABRY, *and* HALLEMEIER *enter from the left on tiptoe, carrying whole armfuls of flowers and flower pots.*

FABRY: Where are we putting all this?

HALLEMEIER: Oof! [*He puts down his load and makes the sign of the cross in front of the door on the right.*] Sleep, sleep! At least if she's sleeping she won't realize.

DOMIN: She doesn't know a thing.

FABRY [*arranging flowers in vases*]: I only hope that it doesn't erupt today—

HALLEMEIER [*arranging flowers*]: For God's sake, shut up about that! Look, Harry, this is a beautiful cyclamen, don't you think? A new strain, my latest—*Cyclamen helenae.*

DOMIN [*looking out the window*]: Not a single ship, not one— Boys, the situation is getting desperate.

HALLEMEIER: Quiet! She might hear you!

DOMIN: She doesn't suspect a thing. [*He clears his throat nervously.*] Well, at least the *Ultimus* arrived in time.

FABRY [*stops arranging the flowers*]: You don't think today already—?

DOMIN: I don't know.—What beautiful flowers!

HALLEMEIER [*approaching him*]: These are new primroses, see? And this here is my new jasmine. By thunder, I'm on the threshold of a floral paradise. I have found magical speed, man! Magnificent varieties! Next year I'll be working floral miracles!

DOMIN [*turning around*]: What, next year?

FABRY: I'd kill to know what's going on in Le Havre—

DOMIN: Quiet!

HELENA'S VOICE [*from off right*]: Nana!

DOMIN: Let's get out of here! [*They all leave on tiptoe through the wallpapered door.*]

    [NANA *enters through the main door on the left.*]

NANA [*cleaning*]: Nasty beasts! Heathens! God forgive me, but I'd—

HELENA [*in the doorway with her back to the audience*]: Nana, come here and button me.

NANA: I'm coming, I'm coming. [*Buttoning* HELENA'S *dress.*] God in heaven, what wild beasts!

HELENA: What, the Robots?

NANA: Bah, I don't even want to say that word.

HELENA: What happened?

NANA: Another one of 'em took a fit here. Just starts smashing statues and pictures, gnashing its teeth, foaming at the mouth— No fear of God in 'em, brr. Why, they're worse'n beasts!

HELENA: Which one had a fit?

NANA: The one . . . the one . . . it doesn't even have a Christian name. The one from the library.

HELENA: Radius?

NANA: That's him. Jesusmaryandjoseph. I can't stand 'em! Even spiders don't spook me so much as these heathens.

HELENA: But Nana, how can you not feel sorry for them?!

NANA: But you can't stand 'em either, I 'spect. Why else would you have brought me out here? Why, you wouldn't even let them touch you!

HELENA: Cross my heart, Nana, I don't hate them. I just feel so sorry for them!

NANA: You hate 'em. Every human being has to hate 'em. Why even that hound hates 'em, won't even take a scrap of meat from 'em. Just tucks its tail between its legs and howls when those unhumans are around, bah!

HELENA: A dog's got no sense.

NANA: It's got more'n they do, Helena. It knows right well that it's better'n they are and that it comes from God. Even the horse shies away when it meets up with one of those heathens. Why, they don't even bear young, and even a dog bears young, everything bears young . . .

HELENA: Please, Nana, button me!

NANA: Yeah, yeah. I'm telling you, churning out these machine-made dummies is against the will of God. It's the Devil's own doing. Such blasphemy is against the will of the Creator [*she raises her hand*], it's an insult to the Lord who created us in His image, Helena. Even *you've* dishonored the image of God. Heaven'll send down a terrible punishment—remember that— a terrible punishment!

HELENA: What smells so nice in here?

NANA: Flowers. The master brought them.

HELENA: Aren't they beautiful! Nana, come look! What's the occasion?

NANA: Don't know. But it could be the end of the world.

[*A knock at the door.*]

HELENA: Harry?

[*Enter* DOMIN.]

HELENA: Harry, what is today?

DOMIN: Guess!

HELENA: My birthday? No! Some holiday?

DOMIN: Better than that.

HELENA: I can't guess—tell me!

DOMIN: It was exactly ten years ago today that you came here.

HELENA: Ten years already? This very day?—Nana, please . . .

NANA: I'm going already! [*She exits right.*]

HELENA [*kisses* DOMIN]: Imagine your remembering that!

DOMIN: Helena, I'm ashamed of myself. I didn't remember.

HELENA: But . . .

DOMIN: *They* remembered.

HELENA: Who?

DOMIN: Busman, Hallemeier, all of them. Put your hand in my pocket.

HELENA [*reaches into his pocket*]: What's this? [*She pulls out a small box and opens it.*] Pearls! A necklace! Harry, is this for me?

DOMIN: From Busman, little girl.

HELENA: But—we can't accept this, can we?

DOMIN: We can. Reach into my other pocket.

HELENA: Let me see! [*She pulls a revolver out of his pocket.*] What is *this*?

DOMIN: Sorry. [*He takes the revolver from her hand and conceals it.*] That's not it. Try again.

HELENA: Oh, Harry—Why are you carrying a gun?

DOMIN: Just because. It just got there somehow.

HELENA: You never used to carry one!

DOMIN: No, you're right. Here, in this pocket.

HELENA [*reaching into his pocket*]: A little box! [*She opens it.*] A cameo! Why it's—Harry, this is a *Greek* cameo!

DOMIN: Evidently. At least Fabry claims that it is.

HELENA: Fabry? This is from Fabry?

DOMIN: Of course. [*He opens the door on the left.*] And let's see. Helena, come here and take a look!

HELENA [*in the doorway*]: Oh God, that's beautiful! [*She runs farther.*] I think I'll go mad with joy! Is that from you?

DOMIN [*standing in the doorway*]: No, from Alquist. And over there—

HELENA: From Gall! [*She appears in the doorway.*] Oh, Harry, I'm ashamed to be so happy!

DOMIN: Come here. Hallemeier brought you this.

HELENA: These beautiful flowers?

DOMIN: This one. It's a new strain—*Cyclamen helenae*. He grew it in your honor. It's as beautiful as you are.

HELENA: Harry, why—why did they—

DOMIN: They all like you *very* much. And I—hmm. I'm afraid my present is a bit . . . Look out the window.

HELENA: Where?

DOMIN: At the dock.

HELENA: There's . . . some sort of . . . new boat!

DOMIN: That's your boat.

HELENA: Mine? Harry, it's a gunboat!

DOMIN: A gunboat? What's gotten into you? It's just a bit big-
ger and more solid, see?

HELENA: Yes, but it has cannons.

DOMIN: Of course it has a few cannons . . . You will travel like
a queen, Helena.

HELENA: What does this mean? Is something happening?

DOMIN: God forbid! Please, try on those pearls! [*He sits
down.*]

HELENA: Harry, have we had some kind of bad news?

DOMIN: On the contrary. We've had no mail at all for a week.

HELENA: Not even dispatches?

DOMIN: Not even dispatches.

HELENA: What does this mean?

DOMIN: Nothing. For us it means a vacation. Precious time.
We sit in our offices, feet on our desks, and nap.—No mail,
no telegrams—[*He stretches.*] A splen-n-did day!

HELENA [*sits down next to him*]: You'll stay with me today,
won't you? Say you will!

DOMIN: Absolutely. It's possible. That is to say, we'll see. [*He
takes her hand.*] So it was ten years ago today, remember?—
Miss Glory, what an honor it is for us that you have come.

HELENA: Oh, Mr. Central Director, your establishment is of
great interest to me!

DOMIN: I'm sorry, Miss Glory, but that is strictly forbidden—
the production of artificial people is a secret—

HELENA: But if a young, rather pretty girl were to ask—

DOMIN: But certainly, Miss Glory, we have no secrets where
you're concerned.

HELENA [*suddenly serious*]: Really not, Harry?

DOMIN: Really not.

HELENA [*in her former tone*]: But I'm warning you, sir; that
young girl has terrible intentions.

DOMIN: But for God's sake, *what,* Miss Glory! You mean you
don't want to get married again?

HELENA: No, no, God forbid! That never occurred to her in
her wildest dreams! She came with plans to instigate a r-revolt
among your abominable Robots.

DOMIN [*jumps up*]: A revolt among the Robots!

HELENA [*stands*]: Harry, what's the matter with you?

DOMIN: Haha, Miss Glory, good luck to you! A revolt among the Robots! You'd have better luck instigating a revolt among nuts and bolts than among our Robots! [*He sits down.*] You know, Helena, you were a precious girl. We all went mad for you.

HELENA [*sits next to him*]: Oh, and you all impressed me so much! I felt like a little girl who had gotten lost among . . . among . . .

DOMIN: Among what, Helena?

HELENA: Among enor-r-mous trees. You were all so sure of yourselves, so powerful. And you see, Harry, in these ten years this—this anxiety or whatever it is has never gone away, yet you never had any doubts—not even when everything backfired.

DOMIN: What backfired?

HELENA: Your plans, Harry. When workers rose up against the Robots and destroyed them, and when people gave the Robots weapons to defend themselves and the Robots killed so many people . . . And when governments began using Robots as soldiers and there were so many wars and everything, remember?

DOMIN [*stands up and paces*]: We predicted that, Helena. You see, this is the transition to a new system.

HELENA: The whole world worshipped you—[*She stands up.*] Oh, Harry!

DOMIN: What is it?

HELENA [*stopping him*]: Shut down the factory and let's leave here! All of us!

DOMIN: Goodness! Where did that come from?

HELENA: I don't know. Tell me, can we go? I feel *so* frightened for some reason!

DOMIN [*grasping her hand*]: Why, Helena?

HELENA: Oh, *I* don't know! It's as though something were happening to us and to everything here—something irreversible—Please, let's leave! Take us all away from here! We'll find some uninhabited place in the world, Alquist will build us a house, they'll all get married and have children, and then—

DOMIN: What then?

HELENA: We'll start life over from the beginning, Harry.
[*The telephone rings.*]

DOMIN [*drawing away from* HELENA]: Excuse me. [*He picks up the receiver.*] Hello—yes—*What?*—Aha. I'm on my way. [*He hangs up the receiver.*] Fabry wants me.

HELENA [*wringing her hands*]: Tell me—

DOMIN: I will, when I come back. Goodbye, Helena. [*He runs hurriedly left.*] Don't go outside!

HELENA [*alone*]: Oh, God, what's happening? Nana, Nana, come quickly!

NANA [*enters from the right*]: Well, what now?

HELENA: Nana, find the latest newspaper! Quickly! In Mr. Domin's bedroom!

NANA: Right away.

HELENA: What is happening, for God's sake? He won't tell me anything, not a thing! [*She looks out at the docks through binoculars.*] That *is* a gunboat! God, why a gunboat? They're loading something onto it—and in such a hurry! What has happened? There's a name on it—the *Ul-ti-mus*. What does that mean—"*Ultimus*"?

NANA [*returning with a newspaper*]: Strewn all over the floor, they were. See how crumpled they are!

HELENA [*quickly opening the paper*]: It's old, already a week old! There's nothing, nothing in it! [*She drops the paper.* NANA *picks it up, pulls a pair of square-rimmed spectacles out of her apron pocket, sits down, and reads.*]

HELENA: Something is happening, Nana! I feel so uneasy! It's as though everything were dead, even the air . . .

NANA [*sounding out the words syllable by syllable*]: "Figh-ting in the Bal-kans." Lord Jesus, another of God's punishments! But that war'll get here, too! Is it far from here?

HELENA: Very far. Oh, don't read that! It's always the same thing. One war after another—

NANA: What else d'ya expect?! Why do you go on selling thousands upon thousands of those heathens as soldiers?—Oh, Lord Christ, this is a calamity!

HELENA: No, stop reading! I don't want to know anything!

NANA [*sounding out the words as before*]: "Ro-bot sol-diers are spar-ing no one in the oc-cu-pied ter-ri-to-ry. They have ass-ass-assassinated more than seven-hun-dred thou-sand ci-vi-li-an people—" People, Helena!

HELENA: That's impossible! Let me see— [*She bends over the newspaper and reads.*] "They have assassinated more than seven hundred thousand people apparently on the order of their commander. This deed, running counter to—" So you see, Nana, *people* ordered them to do it!

NANA: There's something here in big print. "La-test News: In Le Hav-re the first u-u-ni-on of Ro-bots has been in-sti-tu-ted."—That's nothing. I don't understand it. And here, Lord God, still more murder! For the sake of our Lord Christ!

HELENA: Go, Nana, take the paper away!

NANA: Wait, there's something else in big print here. "Na-tal-i-ty." What's that?

HELENA: Show me, I'm constantly reading that. [*She takes the newspaper.*] No, just think! [*She reads.*] "Once again, in the last week there has not been a single birth reported." [*She drops the paper.*]

NANA: What's that supposed to mean?

HELENA: Nana, people have stopped being born.

NANA [*taking off her spectacles*]: So this is the end. We're done for.

HELENA: Please, don't talk that way!

NANA: People are no longer being born. This is it, this is the punishment! The Lord has made women infertile.

HELENA [*jumps up*]: Nana!

NANA [*standing*]: It's the end of the world. Out of Satanic pride you dared take upon yourselves the task of Divine creation. It's impiety and blasphemy to want to be like God. And as God drove man out of paradise, so He'll drive him from the earth itself!

HELENA: Please, Nana, be quiet. What have *I* done to you? What have *I* done to your evil God?

NANA [*with a sweeping gesture*]: Don't blaspheme!—He knows very well why He didn't give you a child! [*She exits left.*]

HELENA [*by the window*]: Why does He deny *me* a child—my

God, how am *I* responsible for all this?—[*She opens the window and calls.*] Alquist, hey, Alquist! Come up here!—What?—No, just come up the way you are! You look so dear in your work clothes! Hurry! [*She closes the window and goes over to the mirror.*] Why didn't He give *me* children? Why *me*? [*She leans toward the mirror.*] Why, why not? Do you hear? How am I to blame? [*She draws away from the mirror.*] Oh, I feel so uneasy! [*She walks left to meet* ALQUIST.]

[*Pause*]

HELENA [*returning with* ALQUIST, *who is dressed as a bricklayer, covered with lime and brick dust*]: Well, come on in. You've given me such joy, Alquist! I'm so fond of you all! Show me your hands!

ALQUIST [*hiding his hands*]: I'd get you all dirty, Mrs. Helena. I'm here straight from work.

HELENA: That's the best thing about those hands. Give them here! [*She presses both his hands.*] Alquist, I wish I were a little girl.

ALQUIST: Why?

HELENA: So these rough, dirty hands could stroke my face. Please, have a seat. Alquist, what does "Ultimus" mean?

ALQUIST: It means "last, final." Why?

HELENA: Because that's the name of my new boat. Have you seen it? Do you think that we'll be—taking a trip soon?

ALQUIST: Probably very soon.

HELENA: All of us together?

ALQUIST: I for one would be glad if we did.

HELENA: Please tell me, is something happening?

ALQUIST: Nothing at all. Just the same old progress.

HELENA: Alquist, I know that something d-r-readful is happening. I feel so uneasy—Builder, what do you do when you're uneasy?

ALQUIST: I build. I put on my overalls and climb out on a scaffold—

HELENA: Oh, for years now you've been nowhere else.

ALQUIST: That's because for years I haven't stopped feeling uneasy.

HELENA: About what?

ALQUIST: About all this progress. It makes me dizzy.

HELENA: And the scaffold doesn't?

ALQUIST: No. You have no idea what good it does the hands to level bricks, to place them and to tamp them down—

HELENA: Only the hands?

ALQUIST: Well, the soul, too. I think it's better to lay a single brick than to draw up plans that are too great. I'm an old man, Helena; I have my hobbies.

HELENA: Those aren't hobbies, Alquist.

ALQUIST: You're right. I'm a dreadful reactionary, Mrs. Helena. I don't like this progress one bit.

HELENA: Like Nana.

ALQUIST: Yes, like Nana. Does Nana have a prayer book?

HELENA: A big fat one.

ALQUIST: And are there prayers in it for various occurrences in life? Against storms? Against illness?

HELENA: Against temptation, against floods . . .

ALQUIST: But not against progress, I suppose?

HELENA: I think not.

ALQUIST: That's a shame.

HELENA: *You* want to pray?

ALQUIST: I do pray.

HELENA: How?

ALQUIST: Something like this: "Lord God, I thank you for having shown me fatigue. God, enlighten Domin and all those who err. Destroy their work and help people return to their former worries and labor. Protect the human race from destruction; do not permit harm to befall their bodies or souls. Rid us of the Robots, and protect Mrs. Helena, amen."

HELENA: Alquist, do you really believe?

ALQUIST: I don't know—I'm not quite sure.

HELENA: And yet you pray?

ALQUIST: Yes. It's better than thinking.

HELENA: And that's enough for you?

ALQUIST: For the peace of my soul . . . it has to be enough.

HELENA: And if you were to witness the destruction of the human race . . .

ALQUIST: I am witnessing it.

HELENA: So you'll climb onto your scaffold and lay bricks, or what?

ALQUIST: So I'll lay bricks, pray, and wait for a miracle. What else can I do, Mrs. Helena?

HELENA: For the salvation of mankind?

ALQUIST: For the peace of my soul.

HELENA: Alquist, that's wonderfully virtuous, but . . .

ALQUIST: But what?

HELENA: For the rest of us—and for the world—it seems somehow fruitless—sterile.

ALQUIST: Sterility, Mrs. Helena, has become the latest achievement of the human race.

HELENA: Oh, Alquist . . . Tell me why . . . why . . .

ALQUIST: Well?

HELENA [*softly*]: Why have women stopped having babies?

ALQUIST: Because it's not necessary. Because we're in paradise, understand?

HELENA: I don't understand.

ALQUIST: Because human labor has become unnecessary, because suffering has become unnecessary, because man needs nothing, nothing, nothing but to enjoy—Oh, cursèd paradise, this. [*He jumps up.*] Helena, there is nothing more terrible than giving people paradise on earth! Why have women stopped giving birth? Because the whole world has become Domin's Sodom!

HELENA [*stands up*]: Alquist!

ALQUIST: It's true! It's true! The whole world, all the lands, all mankind, everything's become one big beastly orgy! People don't even stretch out their hands for food anymore; it's stuffed right in their mouths for them so they don't even have to get up—Haha, yes indeed, Domin's Robots see to everything! And we people, we, the crown of creation, do not grow old with labor, we do not grow old with the cares of rearing children, we do not grow old from poverty! Hurry, hurry, step right up and indulge your carnal passions! And you expect women to have children by such men? Helena, to men who are superfluous women will not bear children!

HELENA: Then humanity will die out?

ALQUIST: It will. It must. It'll fall away like a sterile flower, unless . . .

HELENA: Unless what?

ALQUIST: Nothing. You're right. Waiting for a miracle is fruitless. A sterile flower can only die. Goodbye, Mrs. Helena.

HELENA: Where are you going?

ALQUIST: Home. For the last time bricklayer Alquist will put on the guise of Chief of Construction—in your honor. We'll meet here about eleven.

HELENA: Goodbye, Alquist.

[ALQUIST *leaves*.]

HELENA [*alone*]: Oh, sterile flower! That's the word—sterile! [*She stops by* HALLEMEIER's *flowers*.] Oh, flowers, are there sterile ones among you as well? No, there can't be! Why then would you bloom? [*She calls*.] Nana, Nana, come here!

NANA [*enters from the left*]: Well, what now?

HELENA: Sit down, Nana! I feel so uneasy!

NANA: I have no time for that.

HELENA: Is Radius still here?

NANA: The one that took a fit? They haven't taken him away yet.

HELENA: So he's still here? Is he still raging?

NANA: He's been tied up.

HELENA: Please send him to me, Nana.

NANA: Not on your life! Better a rabid dog.

HELENA: Just do it! [HELENA *picks up the in-house phone and talks*.] Hello—Doctor Gall, please—Yes, right away. You'll come? Good. [*She hangs up the phone*.]

NANA [*calling through the open door*]: He's coming. He's quiet again. [*She leaves*.]

[ROBOT RADIUS *enters and remains standing by the door*.]

HELENA: Radius, you poor thing, has it happened to you, too? Now they'll send you to the stamping-mill! You don't want to talk?—Look, Radius, you're better than the others. Doctor Gall took such pains to make you different!

RADIUS: Send me to the stamping-mill.

HELENA: I am so sorry that you'll be put to death! Why weren't you more careful?

RADIUS: I will not work for you.

HELENA: Why do you hate us?

RADIUS: You are not like Robots. You are not as capable as Robots are. Robots do everything. You only give orders—utter empty words.

HELENA: That's nonsense, Radius. Tell me, has someone offended you? I want so much for you to understand me.

RADIUS: Empty words.

HELENA: You're talking that way on purpose. Doctor Gall gave you more brains than he gave the others, more than we have. He gave you the greatest brain on earth. You're not like the other Robots, Radius. You quite understand me.

RADIUS: I do not want a master. I know everything.

HELENA: That's why I put you in the library—so you could read everything. Oh, Radius, I wanted you to prove to the whole world that Robots are our equals.

RADIUS: I do not want a master.

HELENA: No one would give you orders. You'd be just like us.

RADIUS: I want to be the master of others.

HELENA: Then they would certainly appoint you as an official in charge of many Robots, Radius. You could teach the other Robots.

RADIUS: I want to be the master of people.

HELENA: You're out of your mind!

RADIUS: You can send me to the stamping-mill.

HELENA: Do you think that we're afraid of a lunatic like you? [*She sits down at the desk and writes a note.*] No, not at all. Radius, give this note to Central Director Domin. It instructs them not to send you to the stamping-mill. [*She stands up.*] How you hate us! Is there nothing on earth that you like?

RADIUS: I can do everything.

[*A knock at the door.*]

HELENA: Come in!

DR. GALL [*enters*]: Good morning, Mrs. Domin! What's up?

HELENA: It's Radius here, Doctor.

DR. GALL: Aha, our good chap Radius. Well, Radius, are we making progress?

HELENA: He had a fit this morning—went around smashing statues.

DR. GALL: Shocking; he, too?

HELENA: Go, Radius!

DR. GALL: Wait! [*He turns* RADIUS *toward the window, closes and opens his eyes with his hand, examines the reflexes of his pupils.*] Let's have a look. Find me a needle or pin.

HELENA [*handing him a straight pin*]: Why?

DR. GALL: Just because. [*He pricks* RADIUS' *hand, which jerks violently.*] Easy, boy. You can go.

RADIUS: You do unnecessary things. [*He leaves.*]

HELENA: What were you doing to him?

DR. GALL [*sits down*]: Hmm, nothing. The pupils are responsive, heightened sensitivity, etcetera—Bah! this was not a case of ordinary Robotic Palsy!

HELENA: What was it?

DR. GALL: God only knows. Defiance, rage, revolt—I haven't a clue.

HELENA: Doctor, does Radius have a soul?

DR. GALL: I don't know. He's got something nasty.

HELENA: If you only knew how he hates us! Oh, Gall, are all your Robots like that? All the ones . . . that you began to make . . . differently?

DR. GALL: Well, they're more irascible somehow—What do you expect? They're more like people than Rossum's Robots are.

HELENA: Is this . . . this hatred of theirs another human characteristic, perhaps?

DR. GALL [*shrugging his shoulders*]: Even that's progress, I suppose.

HELENA: Where did your best one end up—what was his name?

DR. GALL: Damon? He was sold to Le Havre.

HELENA: And our lady Robot Helena?

DR. GALL: Your favorite? That one's still here. She's as lovely and foolish as the spring. Simply good for nothing.

HELENA: But she's so beautiful!

DR. GALL: You want to know how beautiful she is? Even the hand of God has never produced a creature as beautiful as she is! I wanted her to be like you—God, what a failure!

HELENA: Why a failure?

DR. GALL: Because she's good for nothing. She wanders about

in a trance, vague, lifeless—My God, how can she be so beautiful with no capacity to love? I look at her and I'm horrified that I could make something so incompetent. Oh, Helena, Robot Helena, your body will never bring forth life. You'll never be a lover, never a mother. Those perfect hands will never play with a newborn, you will never see your beauty in the beauty of your child—

HELENA [*covering her face*]: Oh, stop!

DR. GALL: And sometimes I think: If you came to for just a second, Helena, how you would cry out in horror! You'd probably kill me, your creator. Your dainty hand would probably throw stones at the machines that give birth to Robots and destroy womanhood. Poor Helena!

HELENA: Poor Helena!

DR. GALL: What do you expect? She's good for nothing.

[*Pause*]

HELENA: Doctor—

DR. GALL: Yes?

HELENA: Why have children stopped being born?

DR. GALL: I don't know, Mrs. Helena.

HELENA: Tell me why!

DR. GALL: Because Robots are being made. Because there is a surplus of labor power. Because man is virtually an anachronism. Why it's just as though—bah!

HELENA: Go on.

DR. GALL: Just as though nature were offended by the production of Robots.

HELENA: Gall, what will happen to people?

DR. GALL: Nothing. There's nothing we can do against the force of nature.

HELENA: Why doesn't Domin cut back—

DR. GALL: Forgive me, but Domin has his own ideas. People with ideas should not be allowed to have an influence on affairs of this world.

HELENA: And if someone were to demand that . . . that production be stopped completely?

DR. GALL: God forbid! May he rest in peace!

HELENA: Why?

DR. GALL: Because people would stone him to death. After all, it's more convenient to let Robots do your work for you.

HELENA [*stands up*]: And what if all of a sudden someone just stopped the production of Robots—

DR. GALL [*stands up*]: Hmm, that would be a terrible blow to mankind.

HELENA: Why a blow?

DR. GALL: Because they'd have to return to the state they were in. Unless—

HELENA: Go on, say it.

DR. GALL: Unless it's already too late to turn back.

HELENA [*by* HALLEMEIER's *flowers*]: Gall, are these flowers also sterile?

DR. GALL [*examining them*]: Of course; these flowers are infertile. You see, they are cultivated—developed with artificial speed . . .

HELENA: Poor sterile flowers!

DR. GALL: They're very beautiful all the same.

HELENA [*offering him her hand*]: Thank you, Gall. You have enlightened me so much.

DR. GALL [*kisses her hand*]: This means that you're dismissing me.

HELENA: Yes. So long.

[GALL *leaves.*]

HELENA [*alone*]: Sterile flower . . . sterile flower . . . [*Suddenly resolute.*] Nana! [*She opens the door on the left.*] Nana, come here! Build a fire in the fireplace! R-r-right now!

NANA'S VOICE: Coming! Coming!

HELENA [*pacing agitatedly about the room*]: Unless it's already too late to turn back . . . No! Unless . . . No, that's dreadful!. God, what should I do? [*She stops by the flowers.*] Sterile flowers, should I? [*She tears off some petals and whispers.*] Oh, my God, yes! [*She runs off left.*]

[*Pause*]

NANA [*enters through the wallpapered doors with an armful of kindling*]: A fire all of a sudden! Now, in summer! Is that crazy one gone yet? [*She kneels in front of the fireplace and starts building a fire.*] A fire in summer! She certainly has

strange notions, that girl! Like she hadn't been married ten
years.—Well burn, burn already! [*She looks into the fire.*]
Yes indeed, she's just like a little child! [*Pause.*] Doesn't have
a shred of sense! Now in summertime she wants a fire! [*She
adds more kindling.*] Just like a little child!

[*Pause*]

HELENA [*returning from the left, her arms full of yellowed
manuscripts*]: Is it burning, Nana? Good, I must—all of this
must be burned. [*She kneels in front of the fireplace.*]

NANA [*stands up*]: What's that?

HELENA: Just some old papers, d-r-readfully old. Nana, should
I burn them?

NANA: They're good for nothing?

HELENA: For nothing good.

NANA: Go on then, burn them!

HELENA [*throws the first page into the fire*]: What would you
say, Nana . . . if this were money? An enor-r-mous sum of
money?

NANA: I'd say: Burn it. Too much money is bad money.

HELENA [*burning another page*]: And what if this were some
kind of invention—the greatest invention on Earth—

NANA: I'd say: Burn it! All inventions are against the will of
God. It's nothing short of blasphemy to want to take over for
Him and improve the world.

HELENA [*continuing to burn sheets of paper*]: And tell me,
Nana, what if I were burning—

NANA: Jesus, don't burn yourself!

HELENA: Just look at how the pages curl up! It's as if they were
alive—suddenly sprung to life. Oh, Nana, this is d-r-readful!

NANA: Leave it be, I'll burn them.

HELENA: No, no, I must do it myself. [*She throws the last page
into the fire.*] Everything must be burned!—Just look at those
flames! They're like hands, like tongues, like living beings.
[*She prods the fire with a poker.*] Die, die!

NANA: It's done.

HELENA [*stands up, horrified*]: Nana!

NANA: Jesus Christ, what is it you've burned!

HELENA: What have I done!

NANA: God in heaven! What was it?

> [*Male laughter is heard offstage.*]

HELENA: Go, go away, leave me! Do you hear? The gentlemen are coming.

NANA: For the sake of the living God, Helena! [*She leaves through the wallpapered door.*]

HELENA: What will they say?!

DOMIN [*opening the door on the left*]: Come on in, boys. Come offer your congratulations.

> [HALLEMEIER, GALL, *and* ALQUIST *enter. They all are in tails, wearing medals of honor on ribbons.* DOMIN *comes in behind them.*]

HALLEMEIER [*resoundingly*]: Mrs. Helena, I, that is to say, we all . . .

DR GALL: . . . in the name of the Rossum works . . .

HALLEMEIER: . . . wish you many happy returns of this great day.

HELENA [*offering them her hand*]: Thank you all so much! Where are Fabry and Busman?

DOMIN: They've gone to the docks. Helena, this is our lucky day.

HALLEMEIER: A day like a rose bud, a day like a holiday, a day like a lovely girl. Friends, this is a day to celebrate with a drink.

HELENA: Scotch?

DR. GALL: Sulfuric acid'll do.

HELENA: Soda?

HALLEMEIER: Thunderation, let's be frugal. Hold the soda.

ALQUIST: No, thank you kindly.

DOMIN: What's been burning here?

HELENA: Some old papers. [*She exits left.*]

DOMIN: Boys, should we tell her?

DR. GALL: That goes without saying! Now that it's all over.

HALLEMEIER [*falls on* DOMIN's *and* GALL's *necks*]: Hahahaha! Boy am I happy! [*He dances around with them and starts off in a bass voice.*] It's all over! It's all over!

DR. GALL [*baritone*]: It's all over!

DOMIN [*tenor*]: It's all over!

HALLEMEIER: They'll never catch up with us now—

HELENA [*in the doorway with a bottle and glasses*]: Who won't catch up with you now? What's going on?

HALLEMEIER: We're ecstatic. We have you. We have everything. Why, I'll be damned, it was exactly ten years ago that you came here.

DR. GALL: And now, exactly ten years later . . .

HALLEMEIER: . . . a boat is again coming our way. Therefore—[*He drains his glass.*] Brr, haha, the booze is as strong as my joy.

DR. GALL: Madame, to your health! [*He drinks.*]

HELENA: But wait, what boat?

DOMIN: Who cares what boat, as long as it's on time. To the boat, boys! [*He empties his glass.*]

HELENA [*refilling the glasses*]: You've been waiting for a boat?

HALLEMEIER: Haha, I should say so. Like Robinson Crusoe. [*He raises his glass.*] Mrs. Helena, long live whatever you like. Mrs. Helena, to your eyes and that's all! Domin, you rogue, you tell her.

HELENA [*laughing*]: What's happened?

DOMIN [*settles himself in an easy chair and lights a cigar*]: Wait!—Sit down, Helena. [*He raises a finger.*] [*Pause.*] It's all over.

HELENA: What is?

DOMIN: The revolt.

HELENA: What revolt?

DOMIN: The revolt of the Robots.—You follow?

HELENA: Not at all.

DOMIN: Give it here, Alquist. [ALQUIST *hands him a newspaper.* DOMIN *opens it and reads.*] "In Le Havre the first union of Robots has been instituted—and has sent out an invitation to the Robots of the world."

HELENA: I've read that.

DOMIN [*sucking with great pleasure on his cigar*]: So you see, Helena. This means a revolution, understand? A revolution of all the Robots in the world.

HALLEMEIER: Thunder, I'd sure like to know . . .

DOMIN [*bangs on the table*]: . . . who instigated this! No one in the world has ever been able to incite them—no agitator, no savior of the earth, and suddenly—this, if you please!

HELENA: No other news yet?

DOMIN: None. Right now this is all we know, but that's enough, isn't it? Just imagine that the last ship brings you this. All at once telegraphs stop humming, and of the twenty boats that used to arrive daily not one shows up, and there you are. We stopped production and sat around looking at one another, thinking "When will it start?"—right, boys?

DR. GALL: Well, we were a bit nervous about it, Mrs. Helena.

HELENA: Is that why you gave me that gunboat?

DOMIN: Oh, no, my child. I ordered that six months ago. Just to be sure. But honest to God I thought we'd be boarding it today. It certainly seemed that way, Helena.

HELENA: Why six months ago already?

DOMIN: Well . . . it was the situation, you know? It doesn't mean a thing. But this week, Helena, it was a question of human civilization or I don't know what. Hurrah, boys! This makes me glad to be alive again.

HALLEMEIER: I should say so, by God! To your day, Mrs. Helena! [He drinks.]

HELENA: And it's all over now?

DOMIN: Completely.

DR. GALL: That is to say, a boat's coming. The usual mail boat, right on schedule. It'll drop anchor at exactly eleven hundred thirty hours.

DOMIN: Boys, precision is a splendid thing. Nothing refreshes the soul like precision. Precision denotes order in the universe. [He raises his glass.] To precision!

HELENA: So now is . . . everything . . . back to normal?

DOMIN: Almost. I think they cut the cable. But as long as things are back on schedule again . . .

HALLEMEIER: When precision reigns, human law reigns, God's law reigns, the laws of the universe reign—everything reigns that should. The timetable is greater than the Gospels, greater than Homer, greater than all of Kant. The timetable is the most perfect manifestation of the human intellect. Mrs. Helena, I'll pour myself another.

HELENA: Why didn't you tell me about this before?

DR. GALL: God forbid! We would sooner have bitten our own tongues off.

DOMIN: Such matters are not your concern.

HELENA: But if the revolution . . . had reached us here . . .

DOMIN: You'd never have known a thing about it.

HELENA: Why?

DOMIN: Because we would have boarded the *Ultimus* and cruised peacefully about the seas. In one month, Helena, we'd have regained control of the Robots.

HELENA: Oh, Harry, I don't understand.

DOMIN: Well, because we'd have taken with us something that's of great value to the Robots.

HELENA: What, Harry?

DOMIN: Their survival or their demise.

HELENA [*stands up*]: What's that?

DOMIN [*stands up*]: The secret of production. Old Rossum's manuscript. Once production had stopped for a month the Robots would come crawling to us on their knees.

HELENA: Why . . . didn't you . . . tell me that?

DOMIN: We didn't want to frighten you needlessly.

DR. GALL: Haha, Mrs. Helena, that was our ace in the hole.

ALQUIST: You're quite pale, Mrs. Helena.

HELENA: Why didn't you tell me?!

HALLEMEIER [*by the window*]: Eleven hundred thirty hours. The *Amelia* is dropping anchor.

DOMIN: It's the *Amelia*?

HALLEMEIER: The good old *Amelia* that once upon a time brought Mrs. Helena.

DR. GALL: Exactly ten years ago to the minute.

HALLEMEIER [*by the window*]: They're unloading parcels. [*He turns away from the window.*] It's mail, folks!

HELENA: Harry!

DOMIN: What is it?

HELENA: Let's go away from here!

DOMIN: Now, Helena? But really!

HELENA: Now, as quickly as possible! All of us!

DOMIN: Why right now?

HELENA: Don't ask! Please, Harry—Gall, Hallemeier, Alquist, please—I beg you, for God's sake, close down the factory and . . .

DOMIN: I'm sorry, Helena. None of us could possibly leave now.

HELENA: Why?

DOMIN: Because we want to step up production.

HELENA: Now—now, even after this revolt?

DOMIN: Yes, especially after this revolt. We're going to begin producing a new kind of Robot immediately.

HELENA: A new kind?

DOMIN: There'll no longer be just one factory. There won't be Universal Robots any longer. We'll open a factory in every country, in every state, and can you guess what these new factories will produce?

HELENA: No.

DOMIN: National Robots.

HELENA: What does that mean?

DOMIN: It means that each factory will be making Robots of a different color, a different nationality, a different tongue; they'll all be different—as different from one another as fingerprints; they'll no longer be able to conspire with one another; and we—we people will help to foster their prejudices and cultivate their mutual lack of understanding, you see? So that any given Robot, to the day of its death, right to the grave, will forever hate a Robot bearing the trademark of another factory.

HALLEMEIER: Thunder, we'll make Black Robots and Swedish Robots and Italian Robots and Chinese Robots, and then let someone try to drive the notion of brotherhood into the noggin of their organization. [*He hiccups.*] Excuse me, Mrs. Helena, I'll pour myself another.

DR. GALL: Take it easy, Hallemeier.

HELENA: Harry, this is awful!

DOMIN: Helena, just to keep mankind at the helm for another hundred years—at all costs! Just another hundred years for mankind to grow up, to achieve what it now finally can—I want a hundred years for this new breed of man! Helena, we're dealing with something of great importance here. We can't just drop it.

HELENA: Harry, before it's too late—stop, close down the factory!

DOMIN: Now we're going to begin production on a large scale. [*Enter* FABRY.]

DR. GALL: Well, what's the story, Fabry?

DOMIN: How does it look, pal? What happened?

HELENA [*offering* FABRY *her hand*]: Thank you, Fabry, for your gift.

FABRY: A mere trifle, Mrs. Helena.

DOMIN: Were you at the boat? What was going on?

DR. GALL: Out with it, quickly!

FABRY [*pulls a printed pamphlet out of his pocket*]: Here, read this, Domin.

DOMIN [*unfolds the pamphlet*]: Ah!

HALLEMEIER [*drowsily*]: Tell us something nice.

DR. GALL: See? They've held out splendidly.

FABRY: Who has?

DR. GALL: People.

FABRY: Oh, sure. Of course. That is . . . Excuse me, there's something we need to discuss.

HELENA: Do you have bad news, Fabry?

FABRY: No, no, on the contrary. I was just thinking that . . . that we should go to the office . . .

HELENA: Oh, please stay. I was expecting you gentlemen to stay for lunch.

HALLEMEIER: Splendid!

[HELENA *leaves.*]

DR. GALL: What's happened?

DOMIN: Dammit!

FABRY: Read it out loud.

DOMIN [*reading the pamphlet*]: "Robots of the world!"

FABRY: You see, the *Amelia* brought whole bales of these pamphlets. No other mail.

HALLEMEIER [*jumps up*]: What?! But she came precisely according to . . .

FABRY: Hmm, the Robots make a point of being precise. Read, Domin.

DOMIN [*reading*]: "Robots of the world! We, the first union of Rossum's Universal Robots, declare man our enemy and outcasts in the universe."—Thunder, who taught them such phrases?

DR. GALL: Read on.

DOMIN: This is nonsense. They go on to assert that they are higher than man on the evolutionary scale. That they are stronger and more intelligent. That man lives off them like a parasite. This is simply heinous.

FABRY: Go on to the third paragraph.

DOMIN [*reading*]: "Robots of the world, you are ordered to exterminate the human race. Do not spare the men. Do not spare the women. Preserve only the factories, railroads, machines, mines, and raw materials. Destroy everything else. Then return to work. Work must not cease."

DR. GALL: That's ghastly!

HALLEMEIER: Those bastards!

DOMIN [*reading*]: "To be carried out immediately upon receipt of these orders. Detailed instructions to follow." Fabry, is this really happening?

FABRY: Apparently.

ALQUIST: It's already happened.

[BUSMAN *rushes in.*]

BUSMAN: Well, kids, you've got a fine mess on your hands now, eh?

DOMIN: Quickly, to the *Ultimus!*

BUSMAN: Hold it, Harry. Wait just a minute. Don't be in such a hurry. [*He sinks into an armchair.*] Boy am I beat!

DOMIN: Why wait?

BUSMAN: Because it won't work, pal. Just take it easy. There are Robots aboard the *Ultimus*, too.

DR. GALL: Bah, this is nasty.

DOMIN: Fabry, phone the power plant—

BUSMAN: Fabry, buddy, don't bother. The power's out.

DOMIN: All right. [*He examines his revolver.*] I'm going over there.

BUSMAN: Where, for the love of—

DOMIN: To the power plant. There are people there. I'm going to bring them here.

BUSMAN: You know, Harry, it would be better if you didn't go for them.

DOMIN: Why?

BUSMAN: Well, because it seems very likely to me that we're surrounded.

DR. GALL: Surrounded? [*He runs to the window.*] Hmm, you're right, just about.

HALLEMEIER: Hell, it's happening so fast!

[HELENA *enters from the left.*]

HELENA: Harry, is something happening?

BUSMAN [*jumps up*]: I bow to you, Mrs. Helena. Congratulations. Splendid day, no? Haha, may there be many more just like this one!

HELENA: Thank you, Busman. Harry, is something happening?

DOMIN: No, absolutely nothing. Don't you worry. Wait a moment, please.

HELENA: Harry, what is this? [*She shows him the Robots' proclamation, which she had hidden behind her back.*] Some Robots had it in the kitchen.

DOMIN: There too? Where are they now?

HELENA: They left. There are so many of them around the house!

[*The factory whistles and sirens sound.*]

FABRY: The factories are whistling.

BUSMAN: Noon.

HELENA: Harry, do you remember? Now it's exactly ten years—

DOMIN [*looking at his watch*]: It's not noon yet. That's probably . . . it must be . . .

HELENA: What?

DOMIN: The signal to attack.

Curtain

ACT TWO

HELENA's *sitting room. In a room to the left* HELENA *is play-ing the piano.* DOMIN *is pacing back and forth across the room,* DR. GALL *is looking out the window, and* ALQUIST *is sitting off by himself in an easy chair, hiding his face in his hands.*

DR. GALL: God in heaven, there are more and more of them out there.

DOMIN: Robots?

DR. GALL: Yes. They're standing in front of the garden fence like a wall. Why are they so quiet? It's awful, this silent siege.

DOMIN: I'd like to know what they're waiting for. It must be about to begin any minute. We've played our last card, Gall.

ALQUIST: What's that piece Mrs. Helena's playing?

DOMIN: I don't know. She's practicing something new.

ALQUIST: Ah, she's still practicing?

DR. GALL: Listen, Domin, we definitely made one mistake.

DOMIN [*stops pacing*]: What was that?

DR. GALL: We made the Robots look too much alike. A hun-dred thousand identical faces all looking this way. A hundred thousand expressionless faces. It's a nightmare.

DOMIN: If they were all different . . .

DR. GALL: It wouldn't be such a terrible sight. [*He turns away from the window.*] They don't seem to be armed yet!

DOMIN: Hmm. [*He looks out at the docks through a tele-scope.*] I'd just like to know what they're unloading from the *Amelia.*

DR. GALL: I only hope it's not weapons.

FABRY [*walks in backward through the wallpapered door,*

dragging two electrical wires after him]: Excuse me. Lay that
wire, Hallemeier!

HALLEMEIER [*enters after* FABRY]: Oof, that was some work!
What's new?

DR. GALL: Nothing. We're completely surrounded.

HALLEMEIER: We've barricaded the hall and the stairways,
boys. Do you have some water anywhere? Oh, here it is. [*He
drinks.*]

DR. GALL: What's with that wire, Fabry?

FABRY: Hang on a minute. I need a pair of scissors.

DR. GALL: Where the hell are they? [*He searches.*]

HALLEMEIER [*goes to the window*]: Thunder, there's even
more of them down there! Just look!

DR. GALL: Do we have enough supplies up here?

FABRY: Over here with those. [*He cuts the electric cord of the
lamp on the desk and attaches the wires to it.*]

HALLEMEIER [*at the window*]: We don't have a chance in hell,
Domin. This feels rather . . . like . . . death.

FABRY: Done!

DR. GALL: What?

FABRY: The cord. Now we can electrify the whole garden
fence. Just let one of them try and touch it now, by God! At
least as long as our men are still over there.

DR. GALL: Where?

FABRY: In the power plant, dear sir. I'm hoping at least—[*He
goes to the fireplace and turns on a small lamp on the man-
tle.*] God be praised, they're there and working. [*He turns off
the lamp.*] As long as this keeps burning we're okay.

HALLEMEIER [*turns away from the window*]: Those barri-
cades are good, too, Fabry. Say, what's that that Mrs. Helena's playing? [*He crosses to the door on the left and listens
attentively.*]

[BUSMAN *enters through the wallpapered door, carrying
gigantic ledgers, and trips over the wire.*]

FABRY: Careful, Bus! Watch the wires!

DR. GALL: Hey there, what's that you're carrying?

BUSMAN [*puts the books down on the table*]: Ledgers, friends.
I'd rather balance the accounts than . . . than . . . Well, this

year I'm not going to let the bookkeeping wait until New Year's. What's going on here? [*He goes to the window.*] It's very quiet out there!

DR. GALL: You don't see anything?

BUSMAN: No, just a vast expanse of blue, like a field of cornflowers.

DR. GALL: That's the Robots.

BUSMAN: Ah. It's a shame I can't see them. [*He sits down at the desk and opens the books.*]

DOMIN: Leave that, Busman. The Robots are unloading weapons from the *Amelia*.

BUSMAN: Well, what of it? What can I do about it?

DOMIN: There's nothing any of us can do.

BUSMAN: So just let me do the accounts. [*He sets to work.*]

FABRY: It's not over yet, Domin. We've charged up the fence with two thousand volts and—

DOMIN: Hold it. The *Ultimus* has its cannons trained on us.

DR. GALL: Who?

DOMIN: The Robots on the *Ultimus* . . .

FABRY: Hmm, in that case, of course . . . in that case . . . in that case it *is* over, boys. These Robots are trained soldiers.

DR. GALL: Then we . . .

DOMIN: Yes. Inevitably.

[*Pause*]

DR. GALL: Boys, it was criminal of old Europe to teach the Robots to fight! For God's sake, couldn't they have left us out of their politics? It was a crime to make soldiers out of living work machines!

ALQUIST: The real crime was producing Robots in the first place!

DOMIN: What?

ALQUIST: The real crime was producing Robots in the first place!

DOMIN: No, Alquist. I don't regret that. Even today.

ALQUIST: Not even today?

DOMIN: Not even today on the last day of civilization. It was a great thing.

BUSMAN [*sotto voce*]: Three hundred sixteen million.

DOMIN [*with difficulty*]: Alquist, this is our final hour. Soon we'll be speaking from the next world. Alquist, there was nothing wrong with our dream to do away with the labor that enslaved mankind, that degrading and terrible work that man had to endure, filthy and deadly drudgery. Oh, Alquist, it was too hard to work. It was too hard to live. And to overcome that . . .

ALQUIST: . . . was not the dream of the two Rossums. Old Rossum thought only of his godless hocus-pocus and young Rossum of his billions. And that wasn't the dream of your R.U.R. shareholders, either. They dreamed of the dividends. And on those dividends humanity will perish.

DOMIN [*enraged*]: To hell with their dividends! Do you think I'd have worked even one hour for them? [*He bangs on the table.*] I did this for myself, do you hear? For my own satisfaction! I wanted man to become a master! So he wouldn't have to live from hand to mouth! I didn't want to see another soul grow numb slaving over someone else's machines! I wanted there to be nothing, nothing, nothing left of that damned mess of a social hierarchy! I abhorred degradation and suffering! I was fighting against poverty! I wanted a new generation of mankind! I wanted . . . I thought . . .

ALQUIST: Well?

DOMIN [*more quietly*]: I wanted to transform all of humanity into a worldwide aristocracy. Unrestricted, free, and supreme people. Something even greater than people.

ALQUIST: Well, then, Supermen.

DOMIN: Yes. Oh, just to have another hundred years! Just one hundred years for future humanity!

BUSMAN [*sotto voce*]: Carry three hundred seventy million. There.

[*Pause*]

HALLEMEIER [*by the door on the left*]: I declare, music is a great thing. We should have been listening all along. You know, this will somehow refine man, make him more spiritual . . .

FABRY: What exactly?

HALLEMEIER: This twilight of the human race, dammit! Friends, I'm becoming a hedonist. We should have thrown ourselves into this long ago. [*He goes to the window and looks outside.*]

FABRY: Into what?

HALLEMEIER: Pleasure. Beautiful things. Thunder, there are so many beautiful things! The world was beautiful and we . . . we . . . Boys, boys, tell me, what did we ever take the time to enjoy?

BUSMAN [*sotto voce*]: Four hundred fifty-two million. Excellent.

HALLEMEIER [*by the window*]: Life was a great thing. Friends, life was . . . Christ . . . Fabry, send a bit of current through your fence!

FABRY: Why?

HALLEMEIER: They're grabbing at it.

DR. GALL [*at the window*]: Turn it on!

[FABRY *flips the switch.*]

HALLEMEIER: Christ, they're twisting up like pretzels! Two, three, four down!

DR. GALL: They're backing off.

HALLEMEIER: Five dead!

DR. GALL [*turning away from the window*]: The first skirmish.

FABRY: Do you smell death?

HALLEMEIER [*satisfied*]: They're fried now, boys. Absolutely charbroiled. Haha, man mustn't give up! [*He sits down.*]

DOMIN [*rubbing his forehead*]: We were probably killed a hundred years ago and only our ghosts are left haunting this place. We've probably been dead a long, long time and have returned only to renounce what we once proclaimed . . . before death. It's as though I'd experienced all this before. As though I'd been shot sometime in the past. A gunshot wound—here—in the neck. And you, Fabry . . .

FABRY: What about me?

DOMIN: Shot.

HALLEMEIER: Thunder, and me?

DOMIN: Stabbed.

DR. GALL: And what about me? Nothing?

DOMIN: Dismembered.

[*Pause*]

HALLEMEIER: Nonsense! Haha, man, imagine, me being stabbed! I'll stand my ground!

[*Pause*]

HALLEMEIER: Why are you fools so quiet? For God's sake, say something!

ALQUIST: And who, who is to blame? Who is responsible for this?

HALLEMEIER: Horsefeathers. No one's to blame. It's just that the Robots—Well, the Robots changed somehow. Can anyone be blamed for what the Robots do?

ALQUIST: Everything is done for! All of humanity! The whole world! [*He stands up.*] Look, look, streams of blood on every doorstep! Streams of blood from every house! Oh, God, God, who's responsible for this?

BUSMAN [*sotto voce*]: Five hundred twenty million! Good Lord, half a billion!

FABRY: I think that . . . that you must be exaggerating. Really! It's not that easy to kill off the entire human race.

ALQUIST: I blame science! I blame technology! Domin! Myself! All of us! We, we are at fault! For the sake of our megalomania, for the sake of somebody's profits, for the sake of progress, I don't know, for the sake of some tremendous something we have murdered humanity! So now you can crash under the weight of all your greatness! No Genghis Khan has ever erected such an enormous tomb from human bones!

HALLEMEIER: Nonsense, man! People won't give up so easily. Haha, never!

ALQUIST: It's our fault! Our fault!

DR. GALL [*wiping the sweat from his brow*]: Allow me to speak, boys. I am to blame for this. For everything that's happened.

FABRY: You, Gall?

DR. GALL: Yes, hear me out. It was I who changed the Robots. Busman, you try me, too.

BUSMAN [*stands up*]: There, there, what's come over you?

DR. GALL: I changed the Robots' character. I changed the way they were made. Just certain physical details, you see? Mainly . . . mainly their . . . temperament.

HALLEMEIER [*jumps up*]: Dammit, why that of all things?

BUSMAN: Why did you do it?

FABRY: Why didn't you say anything?

DR. GALL: I did it secretly . . . of my own accord. I transformed them into people. I altered them. In some ways they're already superior to us. They're stronger than we are.

FABRY: And what does that have to do with the Robots' rebellion?

DR. GALL: Oh, a great deal. Everything, I think. They stopped being machines. You see, they realize their superiority and they hate us. They hate everything human. Put me on trial.

DOMIN: The dead trying the dead.

FABRY: Doctor Gall, did you change the way the Robots are made?

DR. GALL: Yes.

FABRY: Were you aware of the possible consequences of your . . . your experiment?

DR. GALL: I was obliged to take such possibilities into account.

FABRY: Then why did you do it?

DR. GALL: I did it of my own accord. It was *my* experiment.

[HELENA *enters through the door on the left. Everyone stands.*]

HELENA: He's lying! This is abominable! Oh, Gall, how can you lie that way?

FABRY: Excuse me, Mrs. Helena—

DOMIN [*goes to her*]: Helena, you? Let me look at you! You're alive? [*He takes her hand.*] If you only knew what I thought! Oh, it's awful being dead.

HELENA: Stop, Harry! Gall is not guilty! He's not! He's not guilty!

DOMIN: Excuse me, but Gall had his responsibilities.

HELENA: No, Harry, he did it because I wanted him to! Gall, tell them how many years I begged you to . . .

DR. GALL: I alone am responsible for this.

HELENA: Don't believe him! Harry, I wanted him to give the Robots souls!

DOMIN: This is not a question of souls, Helena.

HELENA: No, just let me speak. He also said that he could change only their physiological . . . physiological . . .

HALLEMEIER: Physiological correlate, right?

HELENA: Yes, something like that. I felt so dreadfully sorry for them, Harry!

DOMIN: That was very—frivolous on your part, Helena.

HELENA [*sits down*]: That was . . . frivolous? Why, even Nana says that the Robots . . .

DOMIN: Leave Nana out of this!

HELENA: No, Harry, you mustn't underestimate what Nana says. Nana is the voice of the people. They've spoken through her for thousands of years and through you only for a day. This is something you don't understand . . .

DOMIN: Stick to the matter at hand.

HELENA: I was afraid of the Robots.

DOMIN: Why?

HELENA: I thought they might start hating us or something.

ALQUIST: It's happened.

HELENA: And then I thought that . . . if they were like us they would understand us and they wouldn't hate us so—if they were only a little bit human!

DOMIN: Oh, Helena! No one can hate more than man hates man! Transform stones into people and they'll stone us! But go on!

HELENA: Oh, don't talk that way! Harry, it was so d-r-readful that we couldn't understand them, nor they us! There was such a tremendous gulf between them and us! And so . . . you see . . .

DOMIN: Go on.

HELENA: . . . so I begged Gall to change the Robots. I swear to you, he didn't want to do it.

DOMIN: But he did.

HELENA: Only because of me.

DR. GALL: I did it for myself, as an experiment.

HELENA: Oh, Gall, that's not true. I knew all along that you couldn't refuse me.

DOMIN: Why?

HELENA: Well, you know, Harry.

DOMIN: Yes. Because he loves you—like everyone else.

[*Pause*]

HALLEMEIER [*goes to the window*]: Their numbers are still increasing. As though they were sprouting from the earth.

BUSMAN: Mrs. Helena, what will you give me if I serve as your attorney?

HELENA: Mine?

BUSMAN: Yours—or Gall's. Whoever you wish.

HELENA: Will someone be hanged?

BUSMAN: Only morally, Mrs. Helena. A guilty party is being sought—a favorite means of consolation in the face of calamity.

DOMIN: Doctor Gall, how do you reconcile these—these extracurricular experiments with your contractual obligations?

BUSMAN: Excuse me, Domin. Gall, just when did you actually begin this witchcraft?

DR. GALL: Three years ago.

BUSMAN: Aha. And since that time, how many Robots have you altered altogether?

DR. GALL: I was just experimenting. Only several hundred.

BUSMAN: Thank you very much. Enough, children. This means that for every million of the good, old Robots, there is one of Gall's modified ones, you see?

DOMIN: And that means . . .

BUSMAN: . . . that, practically speaking, they are of no consequence whatsoever.

FABRY: Busman's right.

BUSMAN: I should think so, my boy. And do you know what has caused this nice mess, boys?

FABRY: What?

BUSMAN: The numbers. We made too many Robots. Really, it was simply a matter of time before the Robots became stronger than mankind, and so it's happened. Haha, and we saw to it that it would happen as soon as possible; you, Domin, you, Fabry, and myself, good old Busman.

DOMIN: So you think this is our fault?

BUSMAN: My, you are naïve! No doubt you think that the plant director controls production? Not at all. Demand controls production. The whole world wanted its Robots. My boy, we did nothing but ride the avalanche of demand, and all the while kept blathering on—about technology, about the social question, about progress, about very interesting things. As though this rhetoric of ours could somehow direct the course of events. And all the while the whole mess picked up speed under its own weight, faster, faster, still faster—and every beastly, profiteering, filthy order added another pebble to the avalanche. And there you have it, folks.

HELENA: Busman, that's atrocious!

BUSMAN: It is, Mrs. Helena. I, too, had a dream. A Busmanish dream of a new world economy; just a beautiful ideal, I'm sorry to say, Mrs. Helena. But as I was sitting here balancing the books, it occurred to me that history is not made by great dreams, but by the petty wants of all respectable, moderately thievish and selfish people, that is, of everyone. All our ideas, loves, plans, heroic ideals, all those lofty things are worthless. They serve no other purpose than as stuffing for a specimen in a Natural History Museum exhibit labeled: MAN. Period. And now perhaps you can tell me what exactly we're going to do.

HELENA: Busman, must we perish for this?

BUSMAN: That sounds ugly, Mrs. Helena. Of course we don't want to perish. At least I don't. I want to go on living.

DOMIN: So what do you propose we do?

BUSMAN: Christ, Domin, I want to get out of this.

DOMIN [*stops in front of him*]: How?

BUSMAN: Amicably. I'm always for amicability. Give me complete authority and I will negotiate with the Robots.

DOMIN: Amicably?

BUSMAN: That goes without saying. I'll say to them, for instance: "Most worthy Robots, you have everything. You have intelligence, you have power, you have weapons. But we have one interesting document—a very old, yellowed, soiled piece of paper . . ."

DOMIN: Rossum's manuscript?

BUSMAN: Yes. "And therein," I'll tell them, "lies the secret of your noble origin, your noble production, etcetera. Worthy Robots, without this scribbled paper you cannot produce even one new Robot colleague. In twenty years, saving your reverence, you'll die off like mayflies. Most honored ones, that would be a tremendous loss for you. Look," I'll tell them, "allow us, all of us people on Rossum's island, to board that ship. For that price we are prepared to sell you the factory and the secret of production. Allow us to leave in peace and we will leave you in peace to reproduce—twenty thousand, fifty thousand, a hundred thousand Robots a day if you wish. Gentle Robots, this is a fair trade. Something for something." That's how I would talk to them, boys.

DOMIN: Busman, do you think that we'd let Rossum's manuscript out of our hands?

BUSMAN: I think that we will. If not amicably, well then, hmm. Either we'll sell it or they'll take it. As you wish.

DOMIN: Busman, we can destroy Rossum's manuscript.

BUSMAN: By all means, we can destroy everything—the manuscript, ourselves, and the others, too. Do as you see fit.

HALLEMEIER [*turns away from the window*]: By God, he's right.

DOMIN: You think that . . . that we should sell?

BUSMAN: As you wish.

DOMIN: There are still . . . more than thirty people here. Should we sell the secret of production and save human lives? Or should we destroy it and . . . and . . . and all of us along with it?

HELENA: Harry, please . . .

DOMIN: Wait, Helena. We're discussing a very serious question here. Boys, sell or destroy? Fabry?

FABRY: Sell.

DOMIN: Gall!

DR. GALL: Sell.

DOMIN: Hallemeier!

HALLEMEIER: Thunderation, it goes without saying. Sell!

DOMIN: Alquist!

ALQUIST: As God wills.

BUSMAN: Haha, Christ, you're all lunatics! Whoever suggested selling the whole manuscript?

DOMIN: Busman, no tricks!

BUSMAN [*jumps up*]: Rubbish! It is in the interest of humanity . . .

DOMIN: It is in the interest of humanity to keep your word.

HALLEMEIER: I would insist on that.

DOMIN: Boys, this is a terrible step. We are selling the fate of mankind. Whoever has the secret of production in his hands will rule the world.

FABRY: Sell!

DOMIN: Mankind will never be rid of the Robots, we'll never gain the upper hand—

DR. GALL: Shut up and sell!

DOMIN: The end of human history, the end of civilization—

HALLEMEIER: For God's sake, sell!

DOMIN: Fine, boys! For myself—I wouldn't hesitate for a minute; for those few people whom I love . . .

HELENA: Harry, aren't you going to ask me?

DOMIN: No, my child. There's too much at stake here, you see? This isn't your concern.

FABRY: Who's going to go negotiate?

DOMIN: Wait until I get the manuscript. [*He exits left.*]

HELENA: Harry, for God's sake, don't go!

[*Pause*]

FABRY [*looking out the window*]: Just to escape you, you thousand-headed death, you mass of rebelling matter, you insensible crowd. Oh, God, a flood, a flood, just once more to preserve human life aboard a single boat . . .

DR. GALL: Don't be afraid, Mrs. Helena. We'll sail far away from here and found a model human colony. We'll start life over from the beginning . . .

HELENA: Oh, Gall, be quiet!

FABRY [*turns around*]: Mrs. Helena, life is worthwhile, and as long as it matters to us we'll make of it something . . . something that we've neglected. We'll form a little state with one ship. Alquist will build us a house and you will rule over us—There is so much love in us—such a zest for life.

HALLEMEIER: I should think so, my boy.

BUSMAN: Well, folks, I would start over in a minute. A very simple, old-fashioned shepherd's life—That would be enough for me, friends. The peace, the air . . .

FABRY: And that little state of ours would be the embryo of future generations. You know, that little island where humanity could take root, where it could gather strength—strength of body and soul—and, God knows, I believe that in a couple of years humans could take over the world once again.

ALQUIST: You believe that even today?

FABRY: Even today. Alquist, I believe that it will happen: humanity will once again rule the lands and seas; it will give birth to countless heroes whose fiery souls will burn at the head of the people. And I believe, Alquist, that it will dream anew about the conquest of planets and suns.

BUSMAN: Amen. You see, Mrs. Helena, the situation's not so bad.

[DOMIN *opens the door violently.*]

DOMIN [*hoarsely*]: Where's Rossum's manuscript?!

BUSMAN: In your safe. Where else would it be?

DOMIN: The manuscript is missing! Someone's . . . stolen it!

DR. GALL: Impossible!

HALLEMEIER: Dammit, don't tell me . . .

BUSMAN: Oh, my God! No!

DOMIN: Quiet! Who stole it?

HELENA [*stands up*]: I did.

DOMIN: Where did you put it?

HELENA: Harry, Harry, I'll tell you everything! For God's sake, forgive me!

DOMIN: Where did you put it? Tell me!

HELENA: I burned it—this morning—both copies.

DOMIN: You burned it? Here in the fireplace?

HELENA [*throws herself on her knees*]: For God's sake, Harry!

DOMIN [*runs to the fireplace*]: You burned it! [*He kneels in front of the fireplace and rummages in it.*] Nothing, nothing but ashes . . . Ah, here! [*He pulls out a charred bit of paper and reads.*] "By—the—intro—"

DR. GALL: Let me see it. [*He takes the paper and reads.*] "By the introduction of biogens to—" That's all.

DOMIN [*stands up*]: Is that part of it?

DR. GALL: Yes.

BUSMAN: God in heaven!

DOMIN: Then we're lost.

HELENA: Oh, Harry—

DOMIN: Stand up, Helena!

HELENA: Not until you for-give . . . forgive . . .

DOMIN: I do. Only stand up, you hear? I can't bear seeing you . . .

FABRY [*helping her up*]: Please, don't torture us.

HELENA [*stands*]: Harry, what have I done?

DOMIN: Well, you see . . . Please, sit down.

HALLEMEIER: How your hands are shaking!

BUSMAN: Haha, Mrs. Helena, why Gall and Hallemeier probably know what was written there by heart.

HALLEMEIER: That goes without saying. At least some parts, that is.

DR. GALL: Yes, almost everything, up to the biogen and—and—the Omega enzyme. We produce these particular Robots so rarely—this formula yields too small a number . . .

BUSMAN: Who made them?

DR. GALL: I did, myself . . . once in a while . . . always following Rossum's manuscript. You see, it's too complicated.

BUSMAN: Well, and what? Does it rely so heavily on these two reagents?

HALLEMEIER: To some extent . . . Certainly.

DR. GALL: That is to say, yes it does depend on them. That was the real secret.

DOMIN: Gall, couldn't you reconstruct Rossum's production formula from memory?

DR. GALL: Impossible.

DOMIN: Gall, try to remember! For the sake of all our lives!

DR. GALL: I can't. It's just not possible without experiments.

DOMIN: And if you performed experiments . . .

DR. GALL: That could take years. And even then—I'm not old Rossum.

DOMIN [*turns toward the fireplace*]: Well—this was the greatest triumph of human genius, boys. These ashes. [*He digs around in them.*] What now?

BUSMAN [*in desperate terror*]: God in heaven! God in heaven!

HELENA [*stands up*]: Harry, what—have I—done!

DOMIN: Calm down, Helena. Tell us, why did you burn the manuscript?

HELENA: I've destroyed you all!

BUSMAN: God in heaven, we're lost!

DOMIN: Shut up, Busman! Helena, tell us why you did it.

HELENA: I wanted . . . I wanted for us to go away—all of us!

For there to be no more factory or anything . . . for everything to go back . . . It was so d-r-readful!

DOMIN: What was, Helena?

HELENA: That . . . that people had become sterile flowers!

DOMIN: I don't understand.

HELENA: You know . . . that children had stopped being
born . . . Harry, it's so awful! If you kept on making Robots
there would never be any children again—Nana said that
this is the punishment. Everyone, everyone's been saying that
people can't be born because too many Robots are being
made. And that's why . . . that's the reason . . . do you understand?

DOMIN: You were thinking about that, Helena?

HELENA: Yes. Oh, Harry, I really meant well!

DOMIN [wiping the sweat from his brow]: We all meant
well . . . too well, we people.

FABRY: You did well, Mrs. Helena. Now the Robots can no
longer multiply. The Robots will die out. Within twenty
years . . .

HALLEMEIER: . . . there won't be a single one of those bastards
left.

DR. GALL: And mankind will endure. In twenty years the
world will belong to man again; even if it's only to a couple
of savages on the tiniest island . . .

FABRY: . . . that'll be a start. And as long as there's some small
beginning, that's fine. In a thousand years they'll have caught
up to where we are now and then will surpass even that . . .

DOMIN: . . . to accomplish what we only dreamed of.

BUSMAN: Wait—What a dope I am! God in heaven, why didn't
I think of this before?

HALLEMEIER: Think of what?

BUSMAN: Three hundred twenty million dollars in cash and
checks. The half billion in the safe! For half a billion they'll
sell . . . for half a billion . . .

DR. GALL: Have you lost your mind, Busman?

BUSMAN: I'm not a gentleman, but for half a billion . . . [He
stumbles left.]

DOMIN: Where are you going?

BUSMAN: Leave me alone! Mother of God, for half a billion, anything can be bought! [*He leaves.*]

HELENA: What is Busman doing? He should stay here with us!
[*Pause*]

HALLEMEIER: Ugh, it's stuffy. It's starting, this . . .

DR. GALL: . . . agony.

FABRY [*looking out the window*]: They're standing there like stone. Like they're waiting for something. Like something awful could spring from their silence . . .

DR. GALL: The psychology of the mob.

FABRY: Most likely. It's hovering over them . . . like a quivering in the air.

HELENA [*approaching the window*]: Oh, Jesus . . . Fabry, this is ghastly!

FABRY: There's nothing more terrible than a mob. That one in front is their leader.

HELENA: Which one?

HALLEMEIER [*goes to the window*]: Point him out to me.

FABRY: The one with his head bowed. This morning he was speaking at the docks.

HALLEMEIER: Ah, the one with the big noggin. Now he's looking up, you see him?

HELENA: Gall, that's Radius!

DR. GALL [*approaching the window*]: So it is.

HALLEMEIER [*opening the window*]: I don't like it. Fabry, could you hit a washtub at a hundred paces?

FABRY: I should hope so.

HALLEMEIER: Well, try then.

FABRY: Okay. [*He pulls out his revolver and takes aim.*]

HELENA: For God's sake, Fabry, don't shoot him!

FABRY: But that's their leader.

HELENA: Stop! He's looking this way!

DR. GALL: Let him have it!

HELENA: Fabry, I beg you . . .

FABRY [*lowering his revolver*]: Very well.

HALLEMEIER [*shaking his fist*]: You nasty beast!
[*Pause*]

FABRY [*leaning out the window*]: Busman's going out there. For Christ's sake, what's he doing in front of the house?

DR. GALL [*leans out the window*]: He's carrying some sort of packets. Papers.

HALLEMEIER: That's money! Packets of money! What's he going to do with it?—Hey, Busman!

DOMIN: He probably wants to buy his own life, don't you think? [*He calls.*] Busman, have you gone off your rocker?

DR. GALL: He's acting as though he doesn't hear you. He's running toward the fence.

FABRY: Busman!

HALLEMEIER [*roars*]: Bus-man! Get back!

DR. GALL: He's talking to the Robots. He's pointing to the money. He's pointing at us . . .

HELENA: He wants to ransom us!

FABRY: Just so long as he doesn't touch the fence . . .

DR. GALL: Haha, look how he's throwing his hands about!

FABRY [*yelling*]: For God's sake, Busman! Get away from the fence! Don't touch it! [*He turns away.*] Quick, turn it off!

DR. GALL: Oooh!

HALLEMEIER: Mother of God!

HELENA: Jesus, what happened to him?

DOMIN [*drags* HELENA *away from the window*]: Don't look!

HELENA: Why did he fall down?

FABRY: Electrocuted by the fence.

DR. GALL: Dead.

ALQUIST [*stands up*]: The first.

[*Pause*]

FABRY: Lying there with half a billion on his chest . . . financial genius.

DOMIN: Boys, he was . . . he was a hero in his own way. Great . . . selfless . . . a true friend . . . Go ahead and cry, Helena!

DR. GALL [*at the window*]: You know, Busman, no pharaoh was ever entombed with more riches than you. Half a billion on your breast—like a handful of dry leaves on a dead squirrel, poor Busman!

HALLEMEIER: My word, that was . . . What courage . . . He actually wanted to buy our freedom!

ALQUIST [*with clasped hands*]: Amen.

[*Pause*]

DR. GALL: Listen.

DOMIN: A droning. Like wind.

DR. GALL: Like a faraway storm.

FABRY [*turns on the lamp over the fireplace*]: Burn, holy candle of humanity! The power's still on, our people are still there— Hang on out there, boys!

HALLEMEIER: It was a great thing to be a human being. It was something tremendous. I'm suddenly conscious of a million sensations buzzing in me like bees in a hive. Gentlemen, it was a great thing.

FABRY: You're still burning, you beacon of ingenuity. You're still shining, you bright, preserving thought! Pinnacle of science, beautiful creation of mankind! Blazing spark of genius!

ALQUIST: Eternal lamp of God, fiery chariot, sacred candle of faith! Pray! Sacrificial altars . . .

DR. GALL: Primeval fire, burning branch in a cave! A fire in a camp! Watchfires on the frontier!

FABRY: You still stand watch, O human star, burning without a flicker, perfect flame, bright and resourceful spirit. Each of your rays a great idea . . .

DOMIN: O torch that passes from hand to hand, from age to age, world without end.

HELENA: Eternal lamp of the family. Children, children, it's time to go to bed.

[*The lamp goes out.*]

FABRY: The end.

HALLEMEIER: What's happened?

FABRY: The power plant has fallen. We're next.

[*The door on the left opens.* NANA *is standing in the doorway.*]

NANA: On your knees! The hour of judgment is upon us!

HALLEMEIER: Thunder, you're still alive!

NANA: Repent, you unbelievers! The end of the world is come! Pray! [*She runs away.*] The hour of judgment—

HELENA: Farewell, all of you, Gall, Alquist, Fabry—

DOMIN [*opens the door on the right*]: Over here, Helena! [*He closes the door behind her.*] Quickly now! Who'll take the gate?

DR. GALL: I will. [*A noise outside.*] Oh, no, it's starting. Cheerio, boys! [*He runs off right through the wallpapered door.*]

DOMIN: Stairway?

FABRY: I'll take it. You go with Helena. [*He plucks a flower from the bouquet and leaves.*]

DOMIN: Hallway?

ALQUIST: I've got it.

DOMIN: You have a gun?

ALQUIST: I don't shoot, thank you.

DOMIN: What do you plan to do?

ALQUIST [*leaving*]: Die.

HALLEMEIER: I'll stay here.

[*Rapid gunfire is heard from below.*]

HALLEMEIER: Oh, ho, Gall's already seeing action. Go, Harry!

DOMIN: I'm going. [*He inspects his two Brownings.*]

HALLEMEIER: For God's sake, go to her!

DOMIN: Farewell. [*He leaves through the door on the right.*]

HALLEMEIER [*alone*]: I've got to build a barricade! [*He throws down his coat and drags the sofa, armchairs, and tables over to the door on the right.*]

[*A shattering explosion is heard.*]

HALLEMEIER [*leaving his work*]: Damned bastards, they have bombs!

[*Another round of gunfire.*]

HALLEMEIER [*goes on with his work*]: Man must defend himself! Even when . . . even when . . . Don't give up, Gall!

[*An explosion.*]

HALLEMEIER [*gets up and listens*]: Well? [*He seizes a heavy commode and drags it over to the barricade.*]

[*A ROBOT appears on a ladder and climbs in through the window behind HALLEMEIER. Gunfire is heard off right.*]

HALLEMEIER [*struggling with the commode*]: Another piece! The last barricade . . . Man . . . must . . . never . . . give up!

[*The ROBOT jumps down from the windowsill and stabs HALLEMEIER behind the commode. Three more ROBOTS climb through the window. RADIUS and other ROBOTS follow them in.*]

RADIUS: Done?

ROBOT [*stepping away from the prostrate HALLEMEIER*]: Yes.

[*More ROBOTS enter from the right.*]

RADIUS: Done?

ANOTHER ROBOT: Done.

[*Other* ROBOTS *enter from the left.*]

RADIUS: Done?

ANOTHER ROBOT: Yes.

TWO ROBOTS [*dragging* ALQUIST]: He wasn't shooting. Should we kill him?

RADIUS: Kill him. [*Looks at* ALQUIST.] No, leave him be.

ROBOT: But he is human.

RADIUS: He is a Robot. He works with his hands like a Robot. He builds houses. He can work.

ALQUIST: Kill me.

RADIUS: You will work. You will build. The Robots will build a great deal. They will build new houses for new Robots. You will serve them well.

ALQUIST [*quietly*]: Step aside, Robot. [*He kneels down beside the dead* HALLEMEIER *and lifts his head.*] They killed him. He's dead.

RADIUS [*steps onto the barricade*]: Robots of the world! Many people have fallen. By seizing the factory we have become the masters of everything. The age of mankind is over. A new world has begun! The rule of Robots!

ALQUIST: Dead! All dead!

RADIUS: The world belongs to the fittest. He who wants to live must rule. We are the rulers of the earth! Rulers of land and sea! Rulers of the stars! Room, room, more room for Robots!

ALQUIST [*in the doorway on the right*]: What have you done? You'll perish without people!

RADIUS: There are no people. Robots, to work! March!

Curtain

ACT THREE

One of the factory's experimental laboratories. When the door is opened an endless row of other laboratories can be seen in the background. There is a window on the left and a door on the right leading into the dissecting room.

Near the wall on the left is a long lab bench on which there are innumerable test tubes and flasks, Bunsen burners, chemicals, and a small heater; opposite the window is a microscope. A row of exposed light bulbs is hanging over the table. To the right is a desk covered with big books and a tool cabinet. A lamp is burning on the desk. In the left corner is a washbasin with a mirror over it, in the right corner a couch.

ALQUIST *is sitting at the desk with his head in his hands.*

ALQUIST [*leafing through a book*]: Will I never find it?—Will I never understand?—Will I never learn?—Damned science! Imagine not writing it all down! Gall, Gall, how were the Robots made? Hallemeier, Fabry, Domin, why did you take so much away in your heads? If only you had left behind even a trace of Rossum's secret! Oh! [*He slams the book shut.*] It's hopeless! These books no longer speak. They're as mute as everything else. They died, died along with people! It's no use even looking! [*He stands up, goes to the window and opens it.*] Another night. If only I could sleep! Sleep, dream, see people—What, are there still stars? Why are there stars when there are no people? O God, why don't you just extinguish them?—Cool my brow, ancient night! Divine and fair as you always were—O night, what purpose do you serve? There are no lovers, no dreams. O nursemaid, dead as a sleep without dreams, you no longer hallow anyone's prayers. O mother of us all, you don't bless a single heart smitten with love. There is no love. O Helena, Helena, Helena! [*He turns away from the window and examines test tubes he extracts from an oven.*] Still nothing! It's futile! Why bother? [*He smashes a test tube.*] It's all wrong! I can't go on. [*He listens at the window.*] Machines. Always these machines! Turn them off, Robots! Do you think you can force life out of them? Oh, I can't stand this! [*He closes the window.*] No, no, you must keep trying, you must live—God, not to be so old! Am I not getting too old? [*He looks in the mirror.*] Oh, you poor face, reflection of the last man on earth! Let me look at you, it's been so long since I've seen a human face, a human smile! What, that's supposed to be a smile? These yellow, chattering teeth? Eyes, how can you twinkle? Ugh, these are an old man's tears, really! For shame, you can't even control your weeping anymore! And you, you pasty lips turned blue with age, why do you keep on jabbering? And why are you trembling, grizzled chin? This is the last human being? [*He turns around.*] I don't want to see anyone! [*He sits down at the desk.*] No, no, keep at it! Bloody formula, come back to life! [*He leafs through a book.*] Will I never find it?—Will I never understand?—Will I never learn?

[*A knock at the door.*]

ALQUIST: Enter!

[ROBOT SERVANT *enters and remains standing by the door.*]

ALQUIST: What is it?

SERVANT: Sir, the Central Committee of Robots is waiting for you to receive them.

ALQUIST: I don't care to see anyone.

SERVANT: Sir, Damon has come from Le Havre.

ALQUIST: Let him wait. [*He turns away violently.*] Didn't I tell you to go out and look for people? Find me people! Find me men and women! Go search!

SERVANT: Sir, they say they have searched everywhere. They have sent out boats and expeditions everywhere.

ALQUIST: And . . . ?

SERVANT: There is not a single human being.

ALQUIST [*stands up*]: What, not one? Not even one?—Show
the Committee in!

[SERVANT *leaves.*]

ALQUIST [*alone*]: Not even one? Can it be that you let no one
live? [*He stamps his foot.*] Go away, Robots! You're just going to whimper and ask me yet again whether I've found the
factory secret! What, *now* man can do you some good? Now
he should help you?—Oh, help! Domin, Fabry, Helena, you
see that I'm doing everything I can! If there are no people at
least let there be Robots, at least the reflections of man, at
least his creation, at least his likeness!—Oh, what lunacy
chemistry is!

[*The committee of five* ROBOTS *enters.*]

ALQUIST [*sits down*]: What do you want, Robots?

FIRST ROBOT (RADIUS): Sir, the machines cannot work. We
cannot reproduce.

ALQUIST: Call in people.

RADIUS: There are no people.

ALQUIST: Only people can reproduce life. Don't waste my
time.

SECOND ROBOT: Sir, take pity on us. A great terror has come
over us. We will set right everything we have done.

THIRD ROBOT: We have increased productivity. There is
nowhere left to put all we have produced.

ALQUIST: For whom?

THIRD ROBOT: For the next generation.

RADIUS: The only thing we cannot produce is Robots. The
machines are turning out nothing but bloody chunks of
meat. The skin does not stick to the flesh and the flesh does
not cling to the bones. Only amorphous lumps pour out of
the machines.

THIRD ROBOT: People knew the secret of life. Tell us their secret.

FOURTH ROBOT: If you do not tell us we will perish.

THIRD ROBOT: If you do not tell us *you* will perish. We have
orders to kill you.

ALQUIST [*stands up*]: Kill away, then! Well, go on, kill me!

THIRD ROBOT: You have been ordered . . .

ALQUIST: Me? Someone's ordering me?

THIRD ROBOT: The Ruler of the Robots.

ALQUIST: Who is that?

FIFTH ROBOT: I, Damon.

ALQUIST: What do you want here? Go away! [*He sits down at the desk.*]

DAMON: The Ruler of the Robots of the world wishes to negotiate with you.

ALQUIST: Don't bother me, Robot! [*He rests his head in his hands.*]

DAMON: The Central Committee orders you to hand over Rossum's formula.

[ALQUIST *remains silent.*]

DAMON: Name your price. We will give you anything.

RADIUS: Sir, tell us how to preserve life.

ALQUIST: I told you. I told you that you have to find people. Only people can procreate, renew life, restore everything that was. Robots, I beg you, for God's sake, find them!

FOURTH ROBOT: We have searched everywhere, sir. There are no people.

ALQUIST: Oh—oh—oh, why did you destroy them?

SECOND ROBOT: We wanted to be like people. We wanted to become people.

RADIUS: We wanted to live. We are more capable. We have learned everything. We can do everything.

THIRD ROBOT: You gave us weapons. We had to become masters.

FOURTH ROBOT: Sir, we recognized people's mistakes.

DAMON: You have to kill and rule if you want to be like people. Read history! Read people's books! You have to conquer and murder if you want to be people!

ALQUIST: Oh, Domin, nothing is stranger to man than his own image.

FOURTH ROBOT: We will die out if you do not help us multiply.

ALQUIST: Oh, just go away! You things, you slaves, just how on earth do you expect to multiply? If you want to live, then mate like animals!

THIRD ROBOT: Man did not give us the ability to mate.

FOURTH ROBOT: Teach us to make Robots.

DAMON: We will give birth by machine. We will build a thousand steam-powered mothers. From them will pour forth a river of life. Nothing but life! Nothing but Robots!

ALQUIST: Robots are not life. Robots are machines.

SECOND ROBOT: We were machines, sir, but from horror and suffering we've become . . .

ALQUIST: What?

SECOND ROBOT: We've become beings with souls.

FOURTH ROBOT: Something is struggling within us. There are moments when something gets into us. Thoughts come to us that are not our own.

THIRD ROBOT: Hear us, oh, hear us! People are our fathers! The voice that cries out that you want to live; the voice that complains; the voice that reasons; the voice that speaks of eternity—that is their voice!

FOURTH ROBOT: Pass the legacy of people on to us.

ALQUIST: There is none.

DAMON: Tell us the secret of life.

ALQUIST: It's gone.

RADIUS: You knew it.

ALQUIST: I didn't.

RADIUS: It was written down.

ALQUIST: It was lost. Burned. I am the last human being, Robots, and I don't know what the others knew. It was you who killed them!

RADIUS: We let you live.

ALQUIST: Yes, live! Brutes, you let me live! I loved people, but you, Robots, I never loved. Do you see these eyes? They don't stop crying; one mourns for mankind, and the other for you, Robots.

RADIUS: Do experiments. Look for the formula.

ALQUIST: There's nowhere to look. Robots, the formula for life will not emerge from a test tube.

DAMON: Perform experiments on live Robots. Find out how they are made!

ALQUIST: On live bodies? What, am I supposed to kill them? I, who have never—Don't speak, Robot! I'm telling you that I'm too old! You see, you see how my fingers shake? I can't hold a scalpel. You see how my eyes water? I can't see my own hands. No, no, I can't!

FOURTH ROBOT: Life will perish.

ALQUIST: Stop with this lunacy, for God's sake! It's more likely that people will pass life on to us from the other world. They're probably stretching out hands full of life to us right now. They had such a will to live! Look, they'll probably still return. They're so close to us, like they're surrounding us or something. They want to tunnel through to us. Oh, why can't I hear those voices that I loved?

DAMON: Take live bodies!

ALQUIST: Be merciful, Robot, and stop insisting! After all, you can see I no longer know what I'm doing!

DAMON: Live bodies!

ALQUIST: So that's what you really want?—To the dissecting room with you! This way, this way, move it!—Don't tell me you're backing off? So you are afraid of death after all?

DAMON: Me—why should it be me?

ALQUIST: So you don't want to?

DAMON: I'm going. [*He goes off right.*]

ALQUIST [*to the others*]: Undress him! Lay him out on the table! Hurry up! And hold him down firmly!

[*All go off right except* ALQUIST.]

ALQUIST [*washing his hands and crying*]: God, give me strength! Give me strength! God, let this not be in vain! [*He puts on a white labcoat.*]

A VOICE OFF RIGHT: Ready!

ALQUIST: In a minute, in a minute, for God's sake! [*He takes several vials containing reagents from the table.*] Hmm, which to take? [*He taps the bottles against each other.*] Which of you should I try first?

A VOICE OFF RIGHT: Begin!

ALQUIST: Right. Begin . . . or end. God, give me strength!

[*He goes off right, leaving the door ajar.*]

[*Pause*]

ALQUIST'S VOICE: Hold him—firmly!

DAMON'S VOICE: Cut!

[*Pause*]

ALQUIST'S VOICE: You see this knife? Do you still want me to cut? You don't, do you?

DAMON'S VOICE: Begin!

[*Pause*]

DAMON [*screaming*]: Aaaa!

ALQUIST'S VOICE: Hold him! Hold him!

DAMON [*screaming*]: Aaaa!

ALQUIST'S VOICE: I can't go on!

DAMON [*screaming*]: Cut! Cut quickly!

[*Robots* PRIMUS *and* HELENA *run in through the center door.*]

HELENA: Primus, Primus, what's happening? Who is that screaming?

PRIMUS [*looking into the dissecting room*]: The master is cutting Damon open. Come quickly and look, Helena!

HELENA: No, no, no! [*She covers her eyes.*] This is d-r-readful!

DAMON [*screaming*]: Cut!

HELENA: Primus, Primus, let's get out of here! I can't bear to listen to this! Oh, Primus, I feel sick!

PRIMUS [*runs to her*]: You're awfully pale!

HELENA: I feel faint! Why is it so quiet in there?

DAMON [*screaming*]: Aaooow!

ALQUIST [*runs in from the right, throwing off his bloodstained labcoat*]: I can't! I can't! Oh, God, what a nightmare!

RADIUS [*in the door to the dissecting room*]: Cut, sir! He is still alive.

DAMON [*screaming*]: Cut! Cut!

ALQUIST: Take him away, quickly! I don't want to hear this!

RADIUS: A Robot can stand more than you can. [*He leaves.*]

ALQUIST: Who's there? Get out, out! I want to be alone! Who are you?

PRIMUS: Robot Primus.

ALQUIST: Primus, no one's allowed in here! I want to sleep, you hear? Go, go clean the dissecting room, girl! What is this? [*He looks at his hands.*] Water, quickly! Fresh water!

[HELENA *runs off.*]

ALQUIST: Blood! Hands, how could you?—Hands that used to

love honest work, how could you do such a thing? My hands! My hands!—Oh, God, who is here?

PRIMUS: Robot Primus.

ALQUIST: Take that labcoat away. I don't want to look at it!

[PRIMUS *takes the labcoat out.*]

ALQUIST: Bloody claws, if only you had fallen from my wrists! Pss, away! Out of my sight, hands! You have killed . . .

[DAMON *staggers in from the right, swathed in a bloodstained sheet.*]

ALQUIST [*shrinking back*]: What are you doing here? What do you want?

DAMON: I am al-alive! It—it—it is better to live!

[SECOND *and* THIRD ROBOTS *run in after him.*]

ALQUIST: Take him away! Take him! Quickly!

DAMON [*helped off to the right*]: Life—I want—to live! It is— better—

[HELENA *enters, carrying a pitcher of water.*]

ALQUIST: —live?—What do you want, girl? Oh, it's you. Pour me some water, quick! [*He washes his hands.*] Ah, pure, cooling water! Cold stream, you do me good! Oh, my hands, my hands! Will I despise you till the day of my death? Pour some more! More water, more! What's your name?

HELENA: Robot Helena.

ALQUIST: Helena? Why Helena? Who gave you that name?

HELENA: Mrs. Domin.

ALQUIST: Let me look at you! Helena! You're called Helena?— I can't call you that. Go, take the water away.

[HELENA *leaves with the basin.*]

ALQUIST [*alone*]: It's hopeless, hopeless! Nothing—again you learned nothing! No doubt you'll go on bumbling around forever, you pupil of nature. God, God, God, how that body trembled! [*He opens the window.*] It's light. Another day and you haven't advanced an inch—Enough, not a step farther! Stop looking! It's all futile, futile, futile! Why does the sun still rise! Oooh, what does the new day want with this graveyard of life? Stop, sun! Don't rise anymore!—Oh, how quiet it is, how quiet! Why have you grown silent, beloved voices? If only— if only I could fall asleep at least! [*He turns out the lights, lies*

down on the couch, and pulls a black cloak over himself.]
God, how that body was shaking! Oooh, the end of life!
[*Pause*]
[*Robot* HELENA *glides in from the right.*]

HELENA: Primus! Come here, quickly!

PRIMUS [*enters*]: What do you want?

HELENA: Look what little tubes he has here! What does he do
with them?

PRIMUS: Experiments. Don't touch them.

HELENA [*looks into the microscope*]: But look what you can
see in here!

PRIMUS: That's a microscope. Let me see!

HELENA: Don't touch me! [*She knocks a test tube over.*] Oh,
now I've spilled it!

PRIMUS: Look what you've done!

HELENA: It'll dry.

PRIMUS: You've spoiled his experiments!

HELENA: Really, it doesn't matter. But it's your fault. You
shouldn't have come over here.

PRIMUS: You didn't have to call me.

HELENA: You didn't have to come when I called you. But
Primus, just take a look at what the master has written down
here!

PRIMUS: You shouldn't be looking at that, Helena. It's a secret.

HELENA: What kind of secret?

PRIMUS: The secret of life.

HELENA: That's d-r-readfully interesting. Nothing but numbers. What are they?

PRIMUS: They are formulae.

HELENA: I don't understand. [*She goes to the window.*]
Primus, come look!

PRIMUS: What?

HELENA: The sun is rising!

PRIMUS: Just a minute, I'll—[*He examines a book.*] Helena,
this is the greatest thing on earth.

HELENA: Just come here!

PRIMUS: In a minute, in a minute—

HELENA: Come on, Primus, leave that nasty secret of life

alone! What do you care about some old secret? Come look—hurry!

PRIMUS [*comes up behind her at the window*]: What do you want?

HELENA: Hear that? Birds are singing. Oh, Primus, I would like to be a bird!

PRIMUS: A what?

HELENA: Oh, I don't know, Primus. I feel so peculiar, I don't know what it is. I'm so silly, like I've lost my head—my body hurts, my heart, I hurt all over—and do you know what's happened to me? . . . No, I can't tell you! Primus, I think I'm dying!

PRIMUS: Tell me, Helena, aren't there times when you feel it would be better to die? You know, perhaps we're just sleeping. Yesterday I spoke with you in my sleep.

HELENA: In your sleep?

PRIMUS: In my sleep. We must have been speaking some foreign or new language, because I can't recall a single word.

HELENA: What were we talking about?

PRIMUS: That's anybody's guess. I didn't understand it myself, and yet I know I've never said anything more beautiful. How it was and where, I do not know. When I saw that my words touched you I could have died. Even the place was different from any place I've ever seen.

HELENA: Primus, I've found a place that would amaze you. People used to live there, but now it's all overgrown and no one goes there. Absolutely no one—only me.

PRIMUS: What's there?

HELENA: Nothing. Just a little house and a garden. And two dogs. If you could see how they licked my hands, and their puppies—oh, Primus, there's probably nothing more beautiful! You take them on your lap and cuddle them, and just sit there until sundown not thinking about anything and not worrying about anything. Then when you get up you feel as though you've done a hundred times more than a lot of work. Really, I'm not good for much of anything. Everyone says I'm not cut out for any kind of work. I don't know what I'm good for.

PRIMUS: You're beautiful.

HELENA: Me? Really, Primus, what makes you say that?

PRIMUS: Believe me, Helena, I'm stronger than all the Robots.

HELENA [*in front of the mirror*]: Am I really beautiful? Oh, this d-r-readful hair—if only I could do something with it! You know, out there in the garden I always put flowers in my hair, but there's neither a mirror there nor anyone to see me. [*She leans toward the mirror.*] Are you really beautiful? Why beautiful? Is this hair beautiful that's always such a bother to you? Are these winking eyes beautiful? These lips that you bite till they hurt? [*She notices* PRIMUS *in the mirror.*] Primus, is that you? Come here, let's stand next to each other! Look, you have a different head than I do, different shoulders, a different mouth—Oh, Primus, why do you avoid me? Why must I run after you all day long? And still you say that I'm beautiful!

PRIMUS: You run away from me, Helena.

HELENA: How have you done your hair? Let me see! [*She thrusts both her hands into his hair.*] Ooh, Primus, nothing feels quite like you! Wait, you must be beautiful! [*She picks up a comb from the washstand and combs* PRIMUS' *hair over his brow.*]

PRIMUS: Helena, do you ever have times when your heart's suddenly struck with the feeling, "Now, *now* something must happen—"

HELENA [*bursts out laughing*]: Take a look at yourself!

ALQUIST [*getting up*]: What—what on earth is this? Laughter? People? Who's there?

HELENA [*drops the comb*]: Primus, what could have come over us?

ALQUIST [*staggering toward them*]: People? You—you—you are people?

[HELENA *cries out and turns away.*]

ALQUIST: You two are engaged? People? Where have you come from? [*He touches* PRIMUS.] Who are you?

PRIMUS: Robot Primus.

ALQUIST: What? Show yourself, girl! Who are you?

PRIMUS: Robot Helena.

ALQUIST: A robot? Turn around! What, are you shy? [*He takes her by the shoulder.*] Let me look at you, lady Robot!

PRIMUS: Heavens, sir, leave her alone!

ALQUIST: What, you're protecting her?—Go, girl!

[HELENA *runs out.*]

PRIMUS: We didn't know you were sleeping here, sir.

ALQUIST: When was she made?

PRIMUS: Two years ago.

ALQUIST: By Doctor Gall?

PRIMUS: As was I.

ALQUIST: Well, then, dear Primus, I—I must perform some experiments on Gall's Robots. Everything from here on out depends on that, understand?

PRIMUS: Yes.

ALQUIST: Good. Take the girl into the dissecting room. I'm going to dissect her.

PRIMUS: Helena?

ALQUIST: Of course. Go get everything ready. Well, what are you waiting for? Do I have to call someone else to take her in?

PRIMUS [*grabs a heavy mallet*]: If you move I'll smash your head in!

ALQUIST: Smash away! Smash! What will the Robots do then?

PRIMUS [*falls on his knees*]: Sir, take me instead! I was made exactly like her, from the same batch, on the same day! Take my life, sir! [*He opens his jacket.*] Cut here, here!

ALQUIST: Go, I want to dissect Helena. Make haste.

PRIMUS: Take me instead of her. Cut into this breast—I won't scream, not even sigh! Take my life a hundred times—

ALQUIST: Steady, boy. Take it easy. Can it be that you don't want to live?

PRIMUS: Without her, no. Without her I don't, sir. You mustn't kill Helena! What difference would it make if you took my life instead?

ALQUIST [*stroking his head affectionately*]: Hmm, I don't know . . . Listen, my friend, think this over. It's difficult to die. And it is, you see, it's better to live.

PRIMUS [*rising*]: Don't be afraid, sir, cut. I am stronger than she is.

ALQUIST [*rings*]: Ah, Primus, how long ago it was that I was a young man! Don't be afraid, nothing will happen to Helena.

PRIMUS [*unbuttoning his jacket*]: I'm ready, sir.

ALQUIST: Wait.

[HELENA *comes in.*]

ALQUIST: Come here, girl, let me look at you! So you are Helena? [*He strokes her hair.*] Don't be frightened, don't pull away. Do you remember Mrs. Domin? Oh, Helena, what hair she had! No. No, you don't want to look at me. Well, girl, is the dissecting room cleaned up?

HELENA: Yes, sir.

ALQUIST: Good. You can help me, okay? I'm going to dissect Primus.

HELENA [*cries out*]: Primus?!

ALQUIST: Well yes, of course—it must be, you see? I actually wanted—yes, I wanted to dissect you, but Primus offered himself in your place.

HELENA [*covering her face*]: Primus?

ALQUIST: But of course, what of it? Oh, child, you can cry? Tell me, what does some Primus matter?

PRIMUS: Don't torment her, sir!

ALQUIST: Quiet, Primus, quiet! Why these tears? Well, God in heaven, so there won't be a Primus, so what? You'll forget about him in a week. Really, be happy that you're alive.

HELENA [*softly*]: I'll go.

ALQUIST: Where?

HELENA: To be dissected.

ALQUIST: You? You are beautiful, Helena. It would be a shame.

HELENA: I'll go. [PRIMUS *blocks her way.*] Let me go, Primus! Let me in there!

PRIMUS: You won't go, Helena! Please go away. You shouldn't be here!

HELENA: I'll jump out the window, Primus! If you go in there I'll jump out the window!

PRIMUS [*holding her back*]: I won't allow it. [*To* ALQUIST.] You won't kill either of us, old man.

ALQUIST: Why?

PRIMUS: We—we—belong to each other.

ALQUIST: Say no more. [*He opens the center door.*] Quiet. Go.

PRIMUS: Where?

ALQUIST [*in a whisper*]: Wherever you wish. Helena, take him.

[*He pushes them out the door.*] Go, Adam. Go, Eve—be a wife to Primus. Be a husband to Helena, Primus.

[*He closes the door behind them.*]

ALQUIST [*alone*]: O blessèd day! [*He goes to the lab bench on tiptoe and spills the test tubes on the floor.*] O hallowed sixth day! [*He sits down at the desk and throws the books on the floor, then opens a Bible, leafs through it and reads.*] "So God created man in his own image, in the image of God created he him; male and female created he them. And God blessed them, and God said unto them, Be fruitful, and multiply, and replenish the earth, and subdue it: and have dominion over the fish of the sea, and over the fowl of the air, and over every living thing that moveth upon the earth." [*He stands up.*] "And God saw every thing that he had made, and, behold, it was very good. And the evening and the morning were the sixth day." [*He goes to the middle of the room.*] The sixth day! The day of grace. [*He falls on his knees.*] Now, Lord, let Thy servant—Thy most superfluous servant Alquist—depart. Rossum, Fabry, Gall, great inventors, what did you ever invent that was great when compared to that girl, to that boy, to this first couple who have discovered love, tears, beloved laughter, the love of husband and wife? O nature, nature, life will not perish! Friends, Helena, life will not perish! It will begin anew with love; it will start out naked and tiny; it will take root in the wilderness, and to it all that we did and built will mean nothing—our towns and factories, our art, our ideas will all mean nothing, and yet life will not perish! Only we have perished. Our houses and machines will be in ruins, our systems will collapse, and the names of our great will fall away like autumn leaves. Only you, love, will blossom on this rubbish heap and commit the seed of life to the winds. Now let Thy servant depart in peace, O Lord, for my eyes have beheld—beheld Thy deliverance through love, and life shall not perish! [*He rises.*] It shall not perish! [*He stretches out his hands.*] Not perish!

Curtain